MIRACLE AT COLTS RUN CROSS

BY
JOANNA WAYNE

MILLS & BOON®

First published in Great Britain 2009
Harlequin Mills & Boon Limited,
Eton House, 18-24 Paradise Road, Richmond, Surrey TW9 1SR

© Jo Ann Vest 2008

ISBN: 978 0 263 87347 4

46-1209

Harlequin Mills & Boon policy is to use papers that are natural, renewable and recyclable products and made from wood grown in sustainable forests. The logging and manufacturing processes conform to the legal environmental regulations of the country of origin.

Printed and bound in Spain
by Litografia Rosés S.A., Barcelona

"Put the boys on the phone, or I call in the FBI right now."

Nick's threat was met with silence.

Becky had moved to his side, standing so close she could probably hear the hammering of his heart. She didn't touch him, but somehow it made him stronger just to have her near.

Nick hadn't realised until that moment how tightly he'd been holding on to the phone, as if it were a tenuous tether to his sons.

Becky sank onto the couch. Her shudders dissolved into sobs.

Nick could stand it no longer. He crossed the room and dropped to the sofa beside her. He wound an arm around her shoulders, hoping she wouldn't push him away.

Her head fell to his chest. "Get them back, Nick. Just get them back."

Available in December 2009 from Mills & Boon® Intrigue

Soldier Caged
by Rebecca York
&
Seducing the Mercenary
by Loreth Anne White

Christmas Delivery
by Patricia Rosemoor
&
Captive of the Beast
by Lisa Renee Jones

The Bodyguard's Return
by Carla Cassidy
&
Intimate Enemy
by Marilyn Pappano

Miracle at Colts Run Cross
by Joanna Wayne

Holiday with a Vampire
by Maureen Child & Caridad Piñeiro

Kansas City Christmas
by Julie Miller

Joanna Wayne was born and raised in Shreveport, Louisiana and received her undergraduate and graduate degrees from LSU-Shreveport. She moved to New Orleans in 1984 and it was there that she attended her first writing class and joined her first professional writing organisation. Her first novel was published in 1994.

Now, dozens of published books later, Joanna has made a name for herself as being on the cutting edge of romantic suspense in both series and single-title novels.

She currently resides in a small community forty miles north of Houston, Texas, with her husband. Though she still has many family and emotional ties to Louisiana, she loves living in the Lone Star state. You may write to Joanna at PO Box 265, Montgomery, Texas 77356, USA.

To mothers everywhere who know what it means to love a child more than life itself. And to every woman who's ever found that special man whose love is worth fighting for. Here's to Christmas, miracles and love.

Chapter One

Becky Ridgely grabbed her denim jacket from the hook and swung out the back door. A light mist made the air seem much cooler than the predicted fifty-degree high for the day. The gust of wind that caught her off guard didn't help, but she'd had to escape the house or sink even deeper into the blue funk that had a killer grip on her mood.

In a matter of weeks, her divorce from Nick would be final. Their marriage that had begun with a fiery blast of passion and excitement she'd thought would never cool had dissolved into a pile of ashes.

Nonetheless, Nick Ridgely, star receiver for the Dallas Cowboys, was in her living room on the Sunday before Christmas, as large as life on the new big-screen TV and claiming the attention of her entire family. She could understand it of their twin sons. At eight years of age, Nick was David and Derrick's hero. She'd never take that away from them.

But you'd think the rest of the family could show a little sensitivity for her feelings. But no, even her sister and her mother were glued to the set as if winning were paramount to gaining world peace or at least finding a cure for cancer.

Did no one but her get that this was just a stupid game?

Most definitely Nick didn't. For more than half of every year, he put everything he had into football. His time. His energy. His enthusiasm. His dedication. She and the boys were saddled with the leftovers. Some women settled for that. She couldn't, which is why she'd left him and moved back to the family ranch.

Her family liked Nick. Everyone did. And he was a good husband and father in many ways. He didn't drink too much. He had never done drugs, not even in college when all their friends were trying it.

He disdained the use of steroids and would never use the shortcut to improve performance. He didn't cheat on her, though several gossip magazines had connected him to Brianna Campbell, slut starlet, since they had been separated.

But his one serious fault was the wedge that had driven them apart. Once preparation for football season started, he shut her out of his life so completely that she could have been invisible. Oh, he pretended to listen to her or the boys at times, but it was surface only.

His always-ready excuse was that his mind was on the upcoming season or game. The message was that it mattered more than they did. She'd lived with the rejection as long as she could tolerate it, and then she left.

"Mom."

She turned at the panicked voice of her son Derrick. He'd pushed through the back door and was standing on the top step, his face a ghostly white.

She raced to him. "What's the matter, sweetheart?"

"Dad's hurt."

"He probably just had the breath knocked out of him," she said.

"No, it's bad, Mom. Really bad. He's not moving."

She put her arm around Derrick's shoulder as they hurried back to the family room where the earlier cheers had turned deathly silent.

The screen defied her to denounce Derrick's fears. Nick was on his back, his helmet off and lying at a cockeyed angle beside him. Several trainers leaned over him. A half dozen of his teammates were clustered behind them, concern sketched into their faces.

Becky took a deep breath as reality sank in and panic rocked her equilibrium. "What happened?"

"He went up for the ball and got tackled below the waist," Bart said.

Before her brother could say more, the network flashed the replay. A cold shudder climbed her spine as she watched Nick get flipped in midair. He slammed to the ground at an angle that seemed to drive his head and the back of his neck into the hard turf.

His eyes were open, but he had yet to move his arms or legs. Players from the other team joined the circle of players that had formed around him. A few had bowed in prayer. They all looked worried.

"Those guys know what it means to take a hit like that," her brother Langston said. "No player likes to see another one get seriously hurt."

"Yet they go at each other like raging animals." The frustration had flown from Becky's mouth before she could stop it. The stares of her family bore into her, no doubt mistaking her exasperation for a lack of empathy. But they hadn't lived with Nick's obsession for pushing his mind and body to the limit week after week.

"I only meant that it's almost inevitable that players get hurt considering the intensity of the game."

The family grew silent. The announcer droned on and on about Nick's not moving as the trainers strapped him to a backboard and attached a C-collar to support his neck.

David scooted close to the TV and put his hand on the corner of the screen. "Come on, Dad. You'll be all right. You gotta be all right."

"I got hurt bad the first time I played in a real game," Derrick said. "I wanted to cry, but I didn't 'cause the other players make fun of you if you do."

Becky had never wanted her sons to play football, but had given in to their pleadings this year when they turned eight. Nick had always just expected they'd play and spent half the time he was with them practicing the basic skills of the game. It was yet another bone of contention between them.

They showed the replay again while Nick was taken from the field. All of the announcers were in on the act now, concentrating on the grisly possible outcomes from such an injury.

"The fans would love it if Nick could wave a farewell but he still hasn't moved his arms or legs."

"It doesn't look good. It would be terrible to see the career of a player with Nick Ridgely's talent end like this."

"Did you hear that?" Derrick said. "The announcer said Daddy might not ever play football again."

Becky grabbed the remote and muted the sound.

"They don't know. They're not doctors. Most likely Daddy has a bad sprain."

"Your father's taken lots of blows and he's never let one get the best of him yet," her brother Bart said, trying as Becky had to calm the boys.

"We better get up there and check on him," David said. "He might need us."

"You have school tomorrow," Becky said, quickly squashing that idea.

"We can miss," the boys protested in unison.

"It's only half a day," Derrick said. "A bunch of kids won't even be there. Ellen Michaels left Saturday to go visit her grandmother in Alabama for Christmas."

"You have practice for the church Christmas pageant right after school lets out. Mrs. Evans is counting on you."

Becky knew that missing school in the morning wouldn't be a problem. They would have been out all week had they not lost so many days during hurricane season.

They'd been lucky and hadn't received anything but strong winds and excessive rain from two separate storms that had come ashore to the west of them, but if the school board erred, it was always on the side of caution.

Still, if Nick was seriously hurt, the hospital would be no place for the boys. And if he wasn't, he'd be too preoccupied with getting back in the game to notice.

"You can call Daddy later when he's feeling better."

"But you're going to go to Dallas, aren't you, Momma? Daddy's gonna need somebody there with him."

"I can fly you up in the Cessna," Langston said,

offering his private jet. He'd done that before when Nick had been hurt, once even all the way to Green Bay.

But that was when she and Nick were at least making a stab at the marriage. Things had become really strained between them since the divorce proceedings had officially begun. She doubted he'd want her there now.

"Thanks," she said, "but I'm sure Nick's in good hands."

"Maybe you should hold off on that decision until after you've talked to him," her mother said.

"Right," Bart said. "They'll know a lot more after he's X-rayed." The others in the room nodded in agreement.

Becky left the room when the game got back underway. Anxiety had turned to acid in her stomach, and she felt nauseous as she climbed the stairs and went to her private quarters on the second floor of the big house.

Too bad she couldn't cut off her emotions the way a divorce cut off a marriage, but love had a way of hanging on long after it served any useful purpose. Nick would always be the father of her children, but hopefully one day her love for him would be just a memory.

But she wouldn't go to Nick, not unless he asked her to, and she was almost certain that wasn't going to happen. They'd both crossed a line when the divorce papers had been filed. From now on, the only bond between them was their sons.

BECKY CALLED the hospital twice during the hours immediately following Nick's injury. Once he'd still been in the emergency room. The second time he'd been having X-rays. The only real information she'd received was that he had regained movement in his arms and legs.

Her anxiety level had eased considerably with that bit of news, as had everyone else's in the family. The boys still wanted to talk to him, but she'd waited until they were getting ready for bed before trying to reach him again.

Hopefully by now the doctors would have finished with the required tests and Nick would feel like talking to them. Regardless, Nick would play down the pain when talking to her and especially when talking to the boys.

That was his way. Say the right things. Keep his true feelings and worries inside him. It was a considerate trait in a father. It was a cop-out for a husband.

And bitterness stunk in a wife. It was time she accepted things the way they were and moved past the resentment.

"Can you connect me to the room of Nick Ridgely?" she asked when the hospital operator answered.

"He's only taking calls from family members at this time. I've been told to tell all other callers that he is resting comfortably and has recovered full movement in his arms and legs."

Becky had expected that. No doubt the hospital was being bombarded with calls from reporters. "This is his wife."

"Please wait while I put you through to his room, Mrs. Ridgely."

A female voice answered, likely a nurse. "Nick Ridgely's room. If this is a reporter, shame on you for disturbing him."

"This is Becky Ridgely. I'm calling to check on my husband."

"Oops, sorry. It's just that the reporters keep getting through. You don't know how persistent they can be."

Actually, she did. "Is Nick able to talk?"

"He can, but the doctor wants him to stay quiet. I can give him a message."

"I was hoping he could say a word to his sons. They're really worried about him, and I'm not sure they'll sleep well unless he tells them he's okay."

"He isn't okay. His arms are burning like crazy."

This was definitely not a nurse. "To whom am I speaking?"

"Brianna Campbell."

The name hit like a quick slap to the face. He could have waited until the divorce was final to play hot bachelor. If not for her, then for David and Derrick.

"Do you want to leave a message?"

"Yes, tell Nick he can…" She took a quick breath and swallowed her anger as David returned from the bathroom where he'd been brushing his teeth. "No message." Saved from sounding like a jealous wench by the timely appearance of her son.

"Okay, I'll just tell Nick you called, Mrs. Ridgely."

She heard Nick's garbled protest in the background.

"Wait. He's insisting I hand him the phone."

Nice of him to bother.

"Becky."

Her name was slurred—no doubt from pain meds. Derrick had joined them as well now, and both boys had climbed into their twin beds.

"The boys are worried about you."

"Yeah. I knew they would be. I was just waiting to call until I was thinking and talking a bit straighter. Were they watching the game?"

"They always watch your games, Nick."

"Good boys. I miss them."

So he always said, but she wasn't going there with him right now. "How are you?"

"I have the feeling back in my arms and legs. They burned like they were on fire for a bit, but they're better now. The E.R. doc said that was the neurons firing back up so I figure that's a good sign."

"Is there a diagnosis?"

"They think I have a spinal cord contusion. They make it sound serious, but you know doctors. They like complications and two-dollar terms no one else can understand. I'll be fine."

He didn't sound it. He was talking so slowly she could have read the newspaper between sentences. "Do you feel like saying good-night to David and Derrick?"

"Sure. Put them on. I need some cheering up."

That's what she thought Brianna was for. She put the boys on speakerphone so they could both talk at once. Nick made light of the injury, like she'd known he would, and started joking with the boys as if this was just a regular Sunday night post-game chat.

He loved his sons. He even loved her in his own way. It just wasn't enough. She backed from the room as an ache the size of Texas settled in her heart.

MORNING CAME early at Jack's Bluff Ranch, and the sun was still below the horizon when Becky climbed from her bed. She'd had very little sleep, and her emotions were running on empty. Still she managed a smile as she padded into her sons' room to get them up and ready for school.

"Okay, sleepyheads, time to rock and roll."

"Already?" Derrick groaned and buried his head in his pillow.

David rubbed his eyes with his fists and yawned widely as he kicked off his covers. "How come you always say time to rock and roll when we're just going to school?"

"Tradition. That's what your grandma used to say to me."

"Grandma said that?"

"Yes, she did. "Now up and at 'em. She said that, too. And wear something warm. It's about twenty degrees colder than yesterday."

"I wish it would snow," Derrick said as he rummaged through the top drawer of his chest and came up with a red-and-white-striped rugby shirt.

"It never snows in Colts Run Cross," David said.

"Not never, but rarely," Becky agreed. But a cold front did occasionally reach this far south. Today the high would only be in the mid-forties with a chance of thundershowers.

"Have you talked to Daddy this morning?" Derrick asked.

"No, and I don't think we should bother him with phone calls this early. Now get dressed, and I'll see you at breakfast."

Juanita was already at work in the kitchen and had been for over a half hour. Becky had heard the family cook drive up. She'd heard every sound since about

3:00 a.m. when she'd woken to a ridiculous nightmare about Nick's getting hit so hard his helmet had flown off—with his head inside it.

Crazy, but anxiety had always sabotaged her dreams with weird and frightening images. Some people smoked cigarettes or drank or got hives when they were worried. She had nightmares. Over the last ten years, Nick had starred in about ninety-nine percent of them.

Juanita was sliding thick slices of bacon into a large skillet when Becky strode into the kitchen in her pink sweats and fuzzy slippers and poured herself a bracing cup of hot coffee.

The usually jovial Juanita stopped the task and stared soulfully at Becky. "I'm sorry to hear about Nick."

"Thanks." She hoped she would let it go at that.

"I brought the newspaper in. Nick's picture is on the front page."

The front page and no doubt all the morning newscasts, as well. Nick would be the main topic of conversation at half the breakfast tables in Texas this morning.

"The article said he may be out for the rest of the season," Juanita said.

"The rest of the season could be only a game or two depending on whether or not Dallas wins its play-off games, but I don't think anyone knows how long Nick will be on injured reserve."

"I'm sure the boys are upset."

"They talked to him last night, and he assured them he was fine. So I'd appreciate if you didn't mention the article in the paper. They need to go to school and concentrate on their studies."

"Kids at school will talk," Juanita said. "Maybe it

would be best if you show them the article and prepare them."

Becky sighed. "You're right. I should have thought of that myself."

Juanita had been with them so long that she seemed like an extension of the family. She fit right in with the Collingsworth clan, none of whom had ever strayed far from Colts Run Cross.

And if Juanita had been helpful before, she'd been a godsend since Becky's mother, Lenora, had started filling in as CEO for Becky's grandfather, Jeremiah, after his stroke. Thankfully he was back in the office a few days a week now, and Lenora was completing some projects she'd started and easing her way out of the job that would eventually go to Langston. As Jeremiah said, he had oil in his blood.

Jack's Bluff was the second largest ranch in Texas. Becky's brothers Bart and Matt managed the ranch, and both had their own houses on the spread where they lived with their wives.

Her youngest brother, Zach, had recently surprised them all by falling madly in love with a new neighbor, marrying and also taking his first real job. He was now a deputy, in training for the county's new special crimes unit. He and his wife, Kali, lived on her horse ranch.

And though her oldest brother Langston lived with his family in Houston, close to Collingsworth Oil where he served as president for the company, he had a week-end cabin on the ranch.

Her younger sister, Jaime, who'd never married or apparently given any thought to settling down or taking a serious job, lived in the big house with Becky and the boys, along with Becky's mother, Lenora, and Jeremiah, their grandfather. Jeremiah was currently recovering from a lingering case of the flu that hadn't been deterred by this year's flu shot.

Commune might have been a better term for the conglomeration of inhabitants. Becky hadn't planned to stay forever when she'd left Nick and returned to the ranch, but the ranch had a way of reclaiming its own.

The boys missed their father, but they were happy here. More important, they were safe from the kinds of problems that plagued kids growing up in the city.

Becky took her coffee and walked to the den. Almost impulsively, she reached for the remote and flipped on the TV. She was caught off guard as a picture of Nick with David and Derrick flashed across the screen.

Anger rose in her throat. How dare they put her boys' pictures on TV without her permission? Both she and Nick had always been determined to keep them out of the limelight.

"Nick Ridgely's estranged wife Becky is one of the Collingsworths of Collingsworth Oil and Jack's Bluff Ranch. His twin sons Derrick and David live on the ranch with their mother. There's been no word from them on Nick's potentially career-ending injury."

She heard the back door open and Bart's voice as he called to Juanita about the terrific odors coming from the kitchen. Becky switched off the TV quickly and joined them in the kitchen. It would be nice to make it through breakfast without a mention of Nick, but she knew that was too much to hope for.

The next best thing was to head her family off at the pass and keep them from upsetting Derrick and David with new doubts about their father's condition. Nick had left things on a positive note, and she planned to keep them there.

The phone rang, and she inwardly grimaced. Where there's a way, there would be a reporter with questions. And once they started, there would be no letup. Whether she liked it or not, she and her family, especially her sons, were about to be caught in the brutal glare of the public eye.

BULL STARED in the mirror as he yanked on his jeans. "Hell of a looker you are to be living like this," he muttered to himself. Without bothering to zip his pants, he padded barefoot across the littered floor of the tiny bedroom and down the short hall to the bathroom.

After he finished in the john, he stumbled sleepily to the kitchen, pushed last night's leftovers out of his way and started a pot of coffee. This was a piss-poor way to live but still better than that crummy halfway house he'd been stuck in until last week.

And the price was right. Free, unless you counted the food he donated to the roaches and rats that home-steaded here. The cabin had been in his family for years, but he was only passing through until he came up with a plan to get enough money to start over in Mexico.

His parole officer expected him to get a job. Yeah, right. Everyone was just jumping for joy at the chance to hire a man fresh out of prison for stabbing a pregnant woman while in the throes of road rage. No matter that she deserved it.

He stamped his feet to get his blood moving and fight the chill. The cabin was without any heat except what he could get from turning on the oven, and he didn't have the propane to waste on that. The only reason he had electricity was because he'd worked for the power company in his earlier life just long enough to learn how to connect to the current and steal the watts he needed.

Once the coffee was brewing, he started the daily search for the remote. If he didn't know better, he'd swear the rats hid it every night while he was sleeping. This time it turned up under the blanket he'd huddled under to watch the late show last night.

The TV came to life just as the local station broke in with a news flash. He turned up the volume to get the full story. It was all about Nick Ridgely. Apparently he'd gotten seriously injured in Sunday's game. Like who gave a damn about Nick Ridgely?

They showed a picture of him with his sons. Cute kids. But then they would be. Nick was married to Becky Collingsworth. He still had sordid dreams about her in those short little skirts and sweaters that showed off her perky breasts.

But the bitch had never given him the time of day. The announcer referred to her as Nick's estranged wife. Apparently she'd dumped him. Or maybe he'd dumped her. Either way they were both fixed for life, lived like Texas royalty with money to burn while he lived in this dump. The little money he'd stashed away before prison was nearly gone.

No cash. No job. Nothing but a parole officer who kept him pinned down like a tiger in a cage.

Bull's muscles tightened as perverted possibilities skittered through his mind. He went back to the kitchen for coffee, took a long sip and cursed himself silently for even considering doing something that could land him right back in prison.

Still the thoughts persisted and started taking definite shape as the image of Nick Ridgely's twin sons seared into his mind.

Chapter Two

"Too bad about your dad."

"Yeah, man. Tough."

Derrick joined the boys entering the school after recess. "I talked to him last night. He'll be back and better than ever."

"That's not what they said on TV this morning."

David pushed into the line beside them. "Yeah, but they don't know. My mother said they're just making news."

"Well, my daddy said neck injuries are the worst kind. Anyway, I'm sorry he got hurt,"

"Me, too," Butch Kelly added. "I'd be scared to death if it was my dad."

"It's not like he's crippled or anything," David said. "He just took a hit."

Janie Thomas squeezed in beside Derrick. "They put your picture on TV, too. My big sister thinks you're cute."

"Yeah, David, you're cute," Derrick mocked, making his voice sound like a girl.

"You look just like me, you clown. If I'm cute, you are, too."

David followed Derrick to their lockers. They were side by side because they were assigned in alphabetical order. He shrugged out of his jacket and took off the Dallas Cowboys cap his dad had gotten signed by all his teammates. Derrick had one, too. His was white. David's was blue. He wore it everywhere he went.

"Are you worried about Daddy?" Derrick asked.

"I am now," David admitted. "Do you think he might really be hurt too bad to ever play again?"

"I don't know. I think we should ask Uncle Langston to fly us to Dallas to check on him."

"Momma said we couldn't go."

"She said we couldn't miss school, but he could fly us up there at noon, and we could be home by bedtime, like he did when he took us to watch Daddy play the Giants back in October."

David shrugged. "Yeah. Maybe, but I bet Momma's still going to say no."

"We ought to call Uncle Langston. He might talk her into it."

"We'd miss practicing for the pageant."

"So what?" Derrick scoffed. "How much practice does it take to be a shepherd?"

"I'm the little drummer boy."

"Big deal. You just follow the music. I say we call him. The worse thing he can do is say no."

"The office won't let us use the phone unless it's an emergency."

"Our daddy might be hurt bad," Derrick said. "That's an emergency."

"You're right. Let's go call Uncle Langston now.

Maybe he'll check us out early, and we won't have to do math."

"I like that plan. I hate multiplication. It's stupid to do all that work when you can just punch it in the calculator and get the answer right away."

The boys went straight to the office. The good news was that Mrs. Gravits, who worked behind the desk, let them use the phone to call their uncle. The bad news was that Langston wasn't in.

They left a message with his secretary saying they really needed to fly to Dallas today.

BECKY DROVE up to the church ten minutes before the scheduled time for practice to end. Several mothers were already waiting, parked in the back lot nearest the educational building. Her friend Mary Jo McFee waved from her car. Becky waved back.

Normally she would have walked over and spent the ten minutes of waiting time chatting, but she knew that conversation today with anyone would mean answering questions about Nick, and she wasn't up to that.

As it was, the phone at the big house had rung almost constantly since breakfast, and Matt had wranglers guarding the gate to keep the media vultures off ranch property. A couple of photographers had almost gotten to the house before they were turned back.

Becky leaned back and tried to relax before she faced her energetic sons who'd no doubt have new questions of their own about their father. Five minutes later, a couple of girls came out of the church. Mary Jo's daughter was one of them.

A couple of boys came next, and less than a minute

later, the rest of the kids came pouring out the door. Some ran to waiting cars; the ones who lived nearby started walking away in small groups.

Two boys climbed on the low retaining wall between the church and the parking lot. A couple of girls pulled books from their book bags and started reading. But there was no sign of David and Derrick.

Becky waited as a steady group of cars arrived to pick up the waiting children. Her cell phone rang just as the last kid left in a black pickup truck.

She checked the ID and decided not to answer when she didn't recognize the caller. Probably yet another reporter, though she had no idea how they kept getting her cell phone number.

She dropped the phone into the compartment between the front seats, her impatience growing thin. Any other day, her sons would have been the first ones out.

The slight irritation turned to mild apprehension when Rachel Evans, the church's part-time youth co-ordinator, stepped out the door and started walking toward the only other car in the parking lot. Rachel was in charge of the practice and never left until all the children had been picked up.

Rachel noticed Becky and changed direction, walking toward her white Mercedes. Becky lowered her window.

"I'm sorry to hear about Nick," Rachel said. "I guess the boys were too upset to come for practice, not that I blame them."

Becky's apprehension swelled. "Weren't they here?"

"No. Some of the boys said they were flying to Dallas to see their father."

"There must be some mistake. The boys were supposed to be here. Why did their friends think they were going to Dallas?"

"They said that their uncle Langston had picked them up and was taking them in his private jet. In fact, Eddie Mason said he saw them getting into their uncle's car."

Langston would never pick up the boys at school without letting her know, much less fly them to Dallas. But maybe he'd tried to get in touch with her and kept getting a busy signal. Maybe he'd left a message and she hadn't gotten it. Maybe…

Rachel was staring at her, probably thinking she was a very incompetent mother not to know where her sons were. "I'll give Langston a call."

Rachel nodded. "I'm sure you'll find this is all just some kind of miscommunication. It frequently happens when everyone is stressed."

Becky nodded as Rachel walked away, no doubt in a hurry to pick up her own toddler daughter from day care. Becky's pulse rate was climbing steadily as she picked up her phone and punched in Langston's private number. She'd about given up hope of his answering when she heard his hello.

"Where are you, Langston?"

"In the office. Why? What's up?"

"It's the boys. Are they with you?"

"No, why would you think they were?"

"I'm at the church to pick them up from pageant practice, but they're not here."

"Maybe they caught a ride home with someone else."

"No, I just talked to Rachel Evans. She said they never showed up."

"Maybe they forgot about practice and got on the school bus."

"If they had, they would have been home before I left to pick them up. Rachel Evans said that some of the boys at practice mentioned that you were flying David and Derrick to Dallas."

"No. I had a message from David asking me to fly them up there, but I only got it about twenty minutes ago. I was in a meeting all day."

The apprehension took full hold now, and Becky started shaking so hard she could barely hold on to the phone. "If you didn't pick them up, who did?"

"Not mother. She's still here at the office. Did you talk to Bart and Matt—or even Zach?"

"No, but they never pick up the boys unless I ask them to. I'm scared, Langston."

"Try to stay calm, Becky. I'm sure they're fine and this is all a harmless mix-up. Call the ranch. See if they're there."

"And if they're not?"

"Then call Zach. Have him meet you at the church, and don't do anything until he gets there. In the meantime, let me know if you hear anything."

Hot tears welled in the back of Becky's eyes, but she willed them to stay there.

Becky called the big house first, just in case the boys had caught a ride back to the ranch. Juanita was the only one there, and just as Becky had feared, the boys weren't home. She hung up quickly and then punched in Zach's number. He was a deputy now, he'd know what to do. He didn't pick up, but she left a frantic message for him to return her call at once.

Her phone rang again, the jangle of it crackling along her frazzled nerves. This time it was Nick. He was the last person she wanted to talk to now. Still, she took the call.

"Becky, it's Nick," he said, identifying himself as if she wouldn't recognize his voice after a decade of marriage. "Where are the boys?"

She heard the panic in his voice and knew he'd heard. "Did Langston call you?"

"I haven't talked to Langston, but this is very important, Becky. Do you know where the boys are? Are they with you?"

Her blood turned to ice. "What's going on, Nick?"

"Are the boys with you?" he asked again with new urgency in his voice.

"No. I'm at the church. I came to pick them up after their practice for the Christmas pageant, but they're not here. They never showed up."

Nick let loose with a string of muttered curses. "Are you by yourself?"

"Yes, but if you have anything to say, just…"

"I got a phone call a few minutes ago. It was from a man claiming he has the boys with him."

"Who?"

"I don't know. All he said was that he'd call back and that I'd best be ready to deal. I think they've been abducted."

No. Her sons couldn't be kidnapped. This couldn't be happening. She couldn't think, couldn't function. Couldn't breathe.

"We have to find them, Nick."

"We will. Just don't fall apart on me, Becky. We can't make any mistakes."

But she was falling apart, more with every agonizing heartbeat. "They'll be afraid. He might…" God, she couldn't let her mind go there or she'd never get through this. "We have to get them back at once. If it takes every penny either of us has, I don't care. I just want David and Derrick back."

"I'm leaving the hospital now. I'll meet you at Jack's Bluff as soon as I can get there."

"Langston can fly up and get you."

"I can get a chartered flight even quicker. Now go home and stay there in case the man calls you."

She swallowed hard. "I'll call Zach."

"I don't want the sheriff's department in on this, Becky. Not them or any other law enforcement agency, at least until after we talk."

"Don't be ridiculous, Nick. Zach can put out an AMBER Alert and have everyone in the state looking for this madman. And for the record, you don't get to call all the shots, even if it is your fault they're missing."

"Don't start with the blame, Becky, not now." His voice broke. He was hurting and probably as scared as she was.

But this was his fault. He was the one in the news, his name and face all over the TV and every newspaper in the state. And it was him the abductor had called for a ransom.

"The caller said that if we go to the cops, he'll…"

Nick stopped, leaving the sentence unfinished, though the meaning was crystal clear even in Becky's traumatized mind. Nausea hit with a vengeance. She dropped the phone, stepped out of the car and threw up in the parking lot. Weak and unnerved, she finally leaned against the car and gulped in a steadying breath of brisk air.

She would find out who took the twins, and whatever it took, she'd get them back. And heaven help Nick Ridgely if he got in her way.

NICK SHIFTED again, trying to find a way to get comfortable in the four-man helicopter he'd hired to fly him directly to the ranch's helipad. Pain shot through his neck and shoulders with each vibration, but no matter how bad it got, he wouldn't go back on the pain meds. He needed his mind perfectly clear to deal with the situation.

Becky had been quick to hurl the blame at him for the twins' abduction. He couldn't fault her for that. She'd always been determined to protect David and Derrick from the notoriety his career had brought him. She wanted them to have a normal life with solid values. She wanted them safe from the kind of sick person who had them now.

According to the attending physician who'd protested his leaving the hospital, his career could be over. Strapped with the fears of the moment, even that seemed inconsequential.

The pilot landed the helicopter approximately one hundred yards from the big house. Nick grabbed his quickly packed duffel bag, thanked the pilot and jumped out. He walked quickly, breaking into a jog as he neared the house.

He'd come by helicopter before. Then the boys had been watching, and the minute the chopper landed they'd raced to greet him. Their absence now sucked the breath from his lungs. By the time he reached the house, Bart and Matt were standing on the porch, their faces more drawn than he'd ever seen them.

He hoped Becky had kept this from the police, but he knew she wouldn't keep it from her family. Nor would he have wanted that. The Collingsworth brothers, the fearsome four as he'd called them when he'd first started dating Becky, were a powerful squad, and he'd be glad to have them on his side.

He put out his hand to shake Matt's as he stepped on the wide front porch, and then his gaze settled on Becky. She was standing just inside the door, her silhouette backlit by the huge, rustic chandelier that dominated the foyer. She looked far more fragile than the last time he'd seen her, the day she'd told him she was through with being his wife.

He ached to take her in his arms, needed that closeness now more than he'd ever needed it before. Her words of blame shot through his mind, and he held back. Rejection from her might annihilate the tenuous hold he had on his own emotions.

"Glad you made it so quickly," Matt said, his voice level and his handshake firm, though the drawn look to his face and the jut of his jaw were clear indicators of his apprehension.

Bart clapped Nick's shoulder. "Have you heard any more from the abductor?"

"Not a word."

"The family's waiting inside," Matt said. "We should join them."

Nick nodded. Becky had left the door by the time they entered. He followed Bart and Matt into the huge den. The family Collingsworth had gathered en masse—except for Langston's daughter, Gina, and the ill Jeremiah—filling the comfortable sofas and chairs.

Becky was standing near the hearth, and the heat from the blaze in the fireplace flushed her face. Her arms were pulled tight across her chest as if she were holding herself together. She looked at him questioningly, and his stomach rolled with a million unfamiliar emotions.

"He hasn't called back," he said, answering her unspoken question.

She started to shake, and he went to her, steadying her in the crook of his arm until she regrouped and pulled away.

Zach stood. It was the first time Nick had seen him in his khaki deputy's uniform, and he was struck with the added maturity the attire provided.

Zach propped a booted foot on the hearth. "We need an action plan."

"I made a fresh pot of coffee," Bart's wife, Jaclyn, said. "I'll get it."

Langston's wife, Trish, handed their six-month-old son, Randy, off to his dad. "I'll help."

"This is what I've pieced together so far," Zach said. "Eddie Mason said that he saw the boys get into a car right after school let out, apparently when they were walking to the church."

"Has anyone talked to Eddie?" Langston asked.

"Not yet. At this point I'm following Nick's instructions to hold off, but I think it's imperative that we get a description of the car."

"I agree," Matt's wife, Shelly, said. "That information could be critical. So is speed in getting the search under way. That's one thing I definitely learned while with the CIA."

Nick's cell phone rang. The room grew deathly quiet.

He checked the caller ID. Unavailable. His hands were clammy as he punched the button to take the call.

"Just listen. No questions."

His gut hardened to a painful knot. There was no mistaking the abductor's voice.

Chapter Three

"Here's the deal. Five million in small denominations, unmarked, and a flight into Mexico on the Collingsworth's private jet."

All doable, though it surprised Nick for the man to mention the private jet. It made him wonder if the man could live in Colts Run Cross. "Before I agree to anything, I want to talk to my sons."

"No can do."

Nick's body flexed involuntarily. "Why not?"

"They're not with me at the moment."

Dread kicked inside him, but it had fury for company. "Either I talk to the boys and know they're safe, or there will be no deal of any kind."

"You're not calling the plays, Ridgely."

"Put the boys on the phone, or I call in the FBI right now." It was a bluff at this point, but he certainly hadn't ruled out that option. His threat was met with silence, a match for the still, breathless tension that surrounded him.

"Screw yourself." The man's voice reverberated with anger.

Nick waited. Angry or not, if the boys were alive and

safe, the guy wouldn't blow this deal by refusing to let him talk to them—not if he was sane. And heaven help them if he wasn't. There would be no way of predicting the behavior of a crazy man.

Becky had moved to his side, standing so close she could probably hear the hammering of his heart. She didn't touch him, but somehow it made him stronger just to have her near.

"I'll call you back in a half hour." He broke the connection before Nick could respond.

Nick hadn't realized until that moment how tightly he'd been holding on to the phone, as if it were a tenuous tether to his sons. He walked to the window and stared out at the wintry view of bare branches mixed with the green needles of the towering pines, keenly aware that everyone in the room was watching and judging his actions.

Before his marriage had hit the rocks, he'd considered himself as an integral part of the close-knit Collingsworth clan. On the last few visits, the tensions between him and Becky had left him feeling as if he were hovering on the outer rim.

Today all he felt was relief that he was among people who loved his sons and whom he knew would put their lives on the line in a second to save them. Still, he was the father. The final responsibility rested with him.

Trish and Jaclyn returned with the coffee. He waited until they'd served it before he delivered the abductor's message—word for word—or as close as he could remember them. No one interrupted, not even Becky, though she seemed to grow more distraught at every syllable he uttered.

She dropped to the sofa next to her mother. Lenora

reached over and took her daughter's hands, cradling them in hers.

"I'm really uneasy with a no-cops policy," Langston said. "There's a lot of knowledge about situations like this that we're not tapping into. I could call Aidan Jefferies. This is out of his jurisdiction, but he's a hell of a homicide detective, and I know he's had experience with abductions as well."

"I think we should let the sheriff's department handle this," Zach said. "We can put out an AMBER Alert, question anyone who may have seen the boys get into the abductor's car and start investigating any child molesters presently living in the area."

Nick's insides coated in acid at the mention of child molesters, though he'd already thought the same. But his gut feeling led him in another direction. "It seems likely that the abduction was a spur-of-the-moment decision spawned by the media attention yesterday, maybe someone desperate for cash."

"That makes sense," Bart agreed. "The man probably saw the boys' picture on TV."

"No sane person would let a picture of Nick and the twins lead them to kidnapping," Matt said.

Nick shoved his hands into his pockets. "That's my concern and the reason I hate to blow off his demand that we not bring in the authorities. The guy could be a mental case tottering on the edge."

"How will the abductor know if you talk to the cops?" Jaime asked. "I mean as long as they don't come roaring out here in squad cars or show up at the door in uniform."

"If we bring in law enforcement, the kidnapping

could get leaked to the media," Nick said. "I don't think we can risk that—at least not yet."

Lenora leaned forward. "But surely it wouldn't hurt for Zach to do some unofficial investigating."

Nick was amazed at how well his mother-in-law was holding up under this. He knew how much she loved David and Derrick, yet she had a quiet strength about her that he envied. Thank God she was here for Becky since his wife didn't seem to want any comfort or reassurance from him.

"I could fly under the radar," Zach answered, "but we've got to agree on what we're doing here."

"I say pay him off, get the boys back and then we hunt the bastard down," Matt said.

"I'd like to see the FBI brought in," Langston countered. "I have connections. I can make a call right now and have someone come out here from the agency. But Nick and Becky are the ones with the deciding votes. I know I'd make the decisions if it was Gina or little Randy here." He kissed the top of his son's head.

"Where is Gina now?" Jaclyn asked. "Does she know about the abduction?"

"Not yet," Trish said. "She's spending the night in Houston with a girlfriend from her high school who's hosting a Christmas party tonight."

"With a protection service secretly watching her and the house she's in," Langston said. "I'm taking no chances until this crazed abductor is apprehended."

"I curse myself a hundred times an hour for not thinking to do that," Nick said.

Jaime walked over and placed a hand on Nick's arm.

"Don't blame yourself for this. How could you possibly have foreseen something so bizarre?"

Jaime was Zach's twin sister. She was the party girl, but Nick had always suspected she had a lot more depth to her than she let on.

"Would you all just stop talking?" Becky said. Her voice broke, and her whole body began to shake. "My boys are missing, and I want them back. I want them home and in their beds. I want…" Her ranting and shudders dissolved into sobs.

Nick could stand it no longer. He crossed the room and dropped to the sofa beside her. He wound an arm around her shoulders, hoping she wouldn't push him away.

Her head fell to his chest. "Get them back, Nick. Just get them back."

"I will." It was a promise he'd keep or die trying.

Lenora got up from her seat on the other side of Becky. "I think we should give Nick and Becky some time alone."

"Sure," Zach said, "but remember that every second counts in a kidnapping."

Nick had never been more aware of anything in his life.

BECKY FELT as if she were suspended in time, stuck in the horrifying moment when Nick had first told her the boys had been abducted. She pulled away from Nick and tried desperately to regain a semblance of control as the others filed from the room. "I can't stand doing nothing, Nick. I need to know that someone is out there looking for David and Derrick."

"The abductor was adamant that we not go to the police."

"And in the meantime, what about my sons? What's happening to them?"

"The kidnapper wants money, Becky. He's made that clear almost from the second he took them. There's no reason for him to hurt them as long as we cooperate."

"Since when do you know so much about kidnappers? Since when do you know about anything except football?"

"Please don't do this, Becky. It won't help us to tear each other down."

His gaze sought out hers, and she turned away, unable to deal with his pain when hers was so intense.

"I know I'm not all that good with reading people," he said, "but I'm convinced this was a spur-of-the-moment decision with the kidnapper. My guess is he's desperate for money. And desperate men commit irrational acts when pushed against the wall. That's why I don't want to push. I just want to give him the money and bring the boys home."

"And you really think you can pull this off without David and Derrick getting hurt?"

"I think working without the cops is our best chance of doing that."

Nick's face was drawn into hard lines that made him look much older than his thirty-two years. It was odd that she'd never thought of him as aging, though she was keenly aware of it in herself. He was constantly in training, keeping up his speed, agility and strength with the rigorous exercise routine that had kept him at the top of his game.

His boyish good looks and charm had come to him naturally and required nothing but his presence to make them work. But even those were lost tonight in the torment that haunted his eyes.

"If he puts the boys on the phone, I want to talk to them," she said.

"I don't know how much time he'll give us with them."

"Then put the phone on speaker."

"He'll be able to tell and will probably think I have a cop listening in."

She knew he was right, and yet the frustration started swelling in her chest again until it felt like her heart might burst from the pressure. "Are you certain you don't know the abductor, Nick, or at least have some idea who he is?"

"Of course not. Why would you think that?"

Actually, she had no idea where that idea had come from, but now that she'd voiced it, it wasn't all that far-fetched. The man had contacted Nick on his cell phone. He'd had to get that number from somewhere.

And he'd known where the boys went to school. She was certain the morning newscast hadn't mentioned that and was pretty sure that none of the others would have given out that type of information.

"Was the voice disguised?"

"I don't think so."

"Did you get any feel for the man's age?"

"No. He's not a kid, but beyond that, it's impossible to say. He tries to sound tough, but his tone wavers at times. So does the timbre, as if he's getting overly excited or nervous and doesn't want me to know it. That's another reason I think he really just wants to get the money and get out. If we convince him we'll coop-erate with him fully, I think this could be over in a matter of hours."

She ached to believe he was right. "Okay, Nick. I'll

agree to holding off on calling the police or the FBI until he calls again. But if we don't talk to the boys, or if he's hurt them in any way, the deal is off."

"That's all I'm asking, Becky."

His cell phone rang again. She tensed, and the quick intake of breath was choking. He shook his head, a signal that it wasn't the kidnapper. The disappointment laid a crushing weight on her chest.

"I can't talk now. I'll have to call you back later."

Probably Brianna. Becky dropped to the sofa and lowered her head, cradling it in her hands as a new wave of vertigo left her too off balance to stand.

Just keep David and Derrick safe, she prayed silently. If she was granted that, she'd never complain about anything again.

DAVID SUCKED the ketchup from a greasy French fry before stuffing it into his mouth. He chewed and swallowed. Momma didn't like for him to talk with his mouth full. "I don't think you really are my daddy's friend," he said, as he dipped the next fry.

"See, that's where you're wrong. I talked to your daddy when I was outside unloading the two-by-fours from the top of my car. He's real eager to see you boys."

Derrick wiped a dab of mayonnaise from his chin and sat his half-eaten cheeseburger in the middle of the paper wrapper he'd spread out in front of him. "Then how come you didn't take us to Uncle Langston like you said you were going to do?"

"I told you, there was a little misunderstanding, but you'll get to see your daddy soon enough, as long as he cooperates."

"What's that supposed to mean?" David drew a circle in his ketchup with his last fry. He always ate his fries first. Then he ate the meat off the burger. He hated buns.

"It means your Dad and I are working out a deal. He comes up with cash. You go home."

The fry slipped from David's finger and plopped into the puddle of ketchup. "Have we been kidnapped?"

"No, no. Nothing like that. This is just a business deal, and you're the collateral."

"How much cash are you trying to get from Daddy?"

"Just a little pocket money. Five million. Do you think you're worth that?"

David choked and had to spit out the fry he was eating. His allowance was only a dollar a week, and when he'd asked for that super skateboard with all the fancy stuff on it the last time they went to Houston, Momma had said it was too expensive. And that didn't cost even a hundred dollars.

He didn't figure anybody had five million dollars except the Queen of England and maybe that woman who wrote the Harry Potter books. He and Derrick were in big trouble. He looked at his twin brother and could tell he was thinking the same thing.

Derrick jumped up from the rickety chair. "I'm getting out of here right now." He sprinted across the room, heading for the back door.

The guy with the dirty denim jacket grabbed his arm and twisted it behind his back until Derrick yelped in pain.

David ran over and kicked the man in his shins. The guy let go of Derrick and grabbed David. "You kick me again, and I'll take a belt to you, you hear me, boy? You won't have an inch of flesh that's not bruised."

"Then don't you hurt my brother."

Surprisingly the guy laughed. "So you two stick together, eh." Then he stopped smiling and his face turned red. "Let's get one thing straight. I don't want to hurt either one of you, but you try anything funny and I'll lock you in the bathroom and leave you there until this deal is done, do you understand?"

"Sure, I understand," Derrick said. "You're a criminal."

"Right, so don't even think of trying to escape. Besides, even if you did escape, you'd be so lost no one would ever find you but the snakes and buzzards."

"You hurt us and my daddy and uncles will kill you," David said. He was trying hard to act like he wasn't afraid, but he was plenty scared. Not for him but for his brother. Derrick didn't like to listen to anybody, and he might do something stupid.

"I'm treating you good, now aren't I?" the man said. "I bought you hamburgers and fries just like you said you wanted."

"Yeah, but you told us we were coming here to meet Uncle Langston so he could fly us to Dallas."

"I lied. Now I'm going to let you talk to your dad, but you have to tell him how good I'm treating you. And that's all you say. Tell him you're fine and that you want to come home. That way he'll close the deal, and this will all be over."

David nodded. He wanted to talk to Daddy. He wanted that real bad. He didn't like being kidnapped, and he didn't like this cabin. He didn't even want to go to visit his dad at the hospital now. He just wanted to go back to Jack's Bluff. But if he made this man mad, he might never get back.

The man took the cell phone from his pocket and started punching the buttons, whistling the same tune he'd been whistling when he'd picked them up in the car. David put his arm around Derrick's shoulders. He'd do what the man said for now, but he'd find a way out of this. Fast. He wasn't missing Christmas.

THIRTY MINUTES later, there was still no return call. Nick paced the floor, the pain from his injury shooting up his back and settling like smoldering embers in his shoulders and neck. He welcomed the pain. It was familiar and deserved. He'd willingly taken the risks that playing ball in the NFL carried with it.

His boys didn't deserve this mess they were in and neither did Becky. She might have turned against him, but she'd always been a terrific mother. She was the mainstay for both his sons—steady, constant, yet filled with a love of life.

The same Becky he'd fallen so madly in love with from the first day he'd spotted her jogging across the campus in a pair of tight blue running shorts and showing off the best pair of legs he'd ever seen. He'd asked her out for beers and pizza that very night. To his utter amazement, she'd said yes.

The phone vibrated in his clammy hand an instant before its piercing ring shattered the ominous silence surrounding them. No ID information. His muscles tensed as he took the call.

"Nice that you're so available these days, Nick.

Who'd have ever thought you could call a famous Dallas Cowboys receiver and get him on the first ring?"

His grip tightened on the phone. "Are my boys with you?"

"Still don't like talking to people like me, though, do you, Nick Ridgely? Your sons are standing next to me. You can have thirty seconds with each boy."

"Their mother wants to speak to them as well."

"Thirty seconds. You guys divvy it up any way you like. Maybe Brianna Campbell can take a turn, too."

Go to hell! The words hammered against Nick's skull, but never left his mouth. The rotten piece of scum held all the power, and he couldn't risk riling him.

"Daddy."

His heart stopped beating for excruciating moments and then slammed into his chest. "Hi, Derrick. Good to hear your voice."

Becky was at his side in an instant, her eyes begging him for reassurance. He nodded but held on to the phone.

"David and I got kidnapped. Momma's gonna be mad 'cause we got in the car with a stranger, but we thought he was Uncle Langston's friend."

"Mom's not mad, son. Are you okay? Has he hurt you?"

"Not really. He didn't buy the kind of hamburgers we like, though, and he doesn't have much of a TV. It gets lines in it all the time."

A sorry TV. Nick swallowed hard as relief rushed through him. If that was their biggest complaint, he'd called this right. The guy wasn't a child molester. Now Nick just had to get the bastard the money and get the boys back before the situation worsened.

"Momma wants to say hello."

Tears filled Becky's eyes as she reached for the phone. "Are you okay, sweetheart?"

Nick could only hear her side of the conversation, but he could hear the relief in her voice when she realized as he had that their sons were apparently unhurt.

"Daddy and I are taking care of everything. You'll be back with us soon." There was a short pause, and then she whispered I love you and was apparently handed off to David.

"No, David, I'm not mad. I just want you home with me. Daddy's fine. He's here at the ranch. You'll see both of us soon. Are you warm? Did you get enough to eat? Okay, you can talk to Daddy. I love you."

She handed Nick the phone. His time was almost up with the boys, but now that he knew they were safe, it was the abductor he wanted to talk to. The quicker they made the exchange of his sons for money, the less likely they'd have complications.

"Satisfied?" the man asked after letting Nick have only a sentence or two with David.

"For now, but I mean what I said that you'd best not hurt them."

"Yeah, big guy. I'm doing my part. Now it's time for you to do yours."

"I'm ready."

"I'll give you twenty-four hours to get the cash together. Let's see, that will make it at 4:00 p.m. tomorrow."

"I won't need that long."

"Let's leave it at that for now. And have the plane ready."

"Where do you want to meet?"

"I'll call you in the morning with the details. And, remember, no cops or you'll be very, very sorry."

"I'm doing this your way, but if you hurt my sons, I swear I'll track you down, tear your heart out and feed it to the livestock."

"Just get the money and the plane."

Nick held on to the phone after the connection was broken, staring into the flames and the crackling logs in the big stone fireplace. His boys were safe, but he wouldn't breathe easy until they were back on the ranch.

He told Becky what the abductor had said. She cringed even though there was basically nothing new in the kidnapper's demands.

"And that's all?" she asked. "We just hand over the money and he releases the boys?"

"Apparently."

"Then we don't need twenty-four hours. The bank knows I'm good for the funds even if I don't have that much in totally liquid assets. If that's not good enough, my brothers and mother will sign any documents the bank requires."

"I told him we'd have the ransom sooner, but I'll get the money," Nick said, his tone more adamant than he'd intended.

"This isn't about you, Nick, and I couldn't care less about some silly pride thing you seem to have going. I just want David and Derrick home—and safe."

"Don't you think that's what I want?"

She shrugged and walked away, stopping to stand near the blazing fire. She warmed her hands before turning to meet his gaze.

"I don't know what you want anymore, Nick. Maybe I never did."

"No, I guess maybe you didn't."

And that summed up their ten years of marriage. Nothing could compare with the torment of the abduction, but still knowing he was losing Becky cut straight to the heart. He might deserve this, but he didn't see how.

Bart stepped into the den. "Mother gave Juanita the week off so that she didn't have to explain to her about the kidnapping, but the ladies made sandwiches and warmed soup. Can I get you some?"

"I can't eat," Becky said, "but we've finished up in here. Tell mother I'm going to my room for a while— and that I really need to be alone."

"Sure."

Being alone was the last thing Nick needed. And oddly, the soup sounded good. "I'll join you. I just need a minute to wash up."

"You're holding your neck at a funny angle," Bart said. "You must still be in a lot of pain from that hit you took yesterday."

"Some, but don't talk about it. I figure if I ignore it, it will give up and go away." He didn't believe that for a second, but still he'd leave the pain meds in his duffel bag. He was in the middle of the biggest game of his life, and he had to be completely alert.

DERRICK LAY in the twin bed and stared into the blackness. It was so dark he couldn't even see David though he was just a few feet away. There was a window, but the weird guy who'd brought them here had nailed boards over it so they couldn't escape while he was sleeping.

This was all Derrick's fault. He should have known Uncle Langston wouldn't send someone to get them who looked like this guy. But then he didn't look so different from some of the cowboys who worked at the ranch. Some of them had tattoos, too, and they were good wranglers and nice people. Uncle Nick and Uncle Matt said so.

Only the guy hadn't mentioned Uncle Langston until Derrick did. He just stopped the car and called them by name. Then Derrick had asked him if he was there to take them to the hangar where Uncle Langston kept his jet. He said yes and told them to get in. Derrick had hopped in first.

All his fault, so he had to come up with a plan to get them out of here before this crazy guy started twisting their arms behind their backs again. Grown men weren't supposed to hurt kids.

Christmas was Friday. Their pageant was Christmas Eve. He had to come up with an escape plan fast.

He was smart for a third grader. He made A's, well except in math. He figured math didn't really matter if you were going to be a football player. He'd never once seen his dad working multiplication problems.

They could blindside the kidnapper and knock him out with a skillet. He'd seen that once on a TV show. Or sneak into his room while he was asleep and tie him up with the sheets. Only he and David were locked in the bedroom, and if they tried to break the door down he'd hear them.

But they could…

He closed his eyes and then opened them suddenly as the plan appeared like magic in his mind. He climbed out of the bed in the dark and felt his way to David's bed, sliding his hands across the covers until his fingers brushed his brother's arm.

"David." He kept his voice low but shook him awake. "We don't have to worry about Daddy getting five million dollars. I know how we can escape."

Chapter Four

As it turned out, getting five million dollars in cash on short notice was more of a problem than any of them had anticipated. Nick had the funds but not in liquid assets. Converting it to cash would incur time that they didn't have.

Finally, it had been Langston who'd arranged the transaction through the business account of Collingsworth Oil. Becky wasn't sure how Langston had explained his need for so much money in small denominations, but apparently he had, or else the bank didn't ask questions of their larger business accounts.

Becky and Nick were on their way into Houston to pick up the money from one of the main branches now. Nick was still in obvious pain from Sunday's injury, so Becky was at the wheel and fighting the noonday traffic. Nick was holding his head at a weird angle and massaging the back of his neck.

"Do you have something to take for the pain?" she asked.

"Back at the ranch, but I'm not taking anything that affects my judgment."

Becky took the freeway exit to the downtown area. The city was decorated for the holidays with huge wreaths on the fronts of buildings and storefronts and holiday displays in all the shop windows. The light changed to red, and she stopped near the corner where a Salvation Army worker was standing by her kettle and ringing a large red bell.

The spirit of the season came crashing down on Becky like blankets of gloom. Ever since the boys were old enough to tear wrapping paper from a present, Christmas had been her favorite time of year. She loved the carols and decorations, the boys' excitement and the traditions.

They always decorated the tree before dinner on Christmas Eve. The entire family took part, but David and Derrick had more fun than anyone even though they spent as much time sneaking fudge from the kitchen as they did hanging ornaments.

Then, as far back as Becky could remember, they'd had hot tamales and Texas chili on Christmas Eve before leaving for the community Christmas pageant at their church. It was the highlight of the evening with even the eggnog, hot chocolate and desserts that followed taking a backseat.

"Derrick has a speaking part in the Christmas pageant, and David plays his drum." She didn't know why she'd blurted that out except that the thought of Christmas without them was unbearable.

"They'll be there for it," Nick said. "The boys will be back with us by tonight."

She wanted desperately to believe that, but the cold, hard knots of doubt wouldn't let go. The light changed again, and she sped through the intersection, eager to get the money in hand.

"I'd like to be here for the pageant," Nick said. "And for Christmas morning, too."

The old resentment surged. "Don't you have a big game in Chicago on Saturday?" Even when he hadn't been cleared to dress out, he'd always traveled with the team.

"I'll miss the game," he said.

"Are you feeling guilty, Nick?"

"I just think it's important that I be here for Christmas this year. Can we just leave it at that?"

She spotted the bank ahead and determinedly forced her bitterness aside. She parked the car in a lot across the street from the bank. Nick paid the attendant while she grabbed the large valises they'd bought for the money and locked the car door. When they left the bank, an armed guard in street clothes would walk them to the car.

"I'll take those," Nick said, joining her and slipping the bags from her arm.

He slung the strap over his left shoulder and linked his right arm with hers. An incredible feeling of déjà vu swept over her. Walking arm in arm with Nick, the valise over his shoulder, a feeling of urgency burned inside both of them.

Like the night they'd rushed to the hospital for the twins to be born. Her water had broken and she'd been propelled into labor with strong contractions that came much faster than normal. Nick had flown into action, trying to be tough but clearly as frightened as she was. But he'd stayed with her every second.

The image of him holding both the boys in his arms

minutes after they were born pushed its way into her mind. His smile. His wet eyes. The tenderness when he'd kissed her and thanked her for giving him the world. She shivered as the memories took hold.

Nick let his hand slip down to encase hers. "It's going to be okay, baby. This is all going to be okay."

But who was Nick to promise a happy ending?

DAVID WAS CURLED UP in a smelly old chair with stains all over it. He looked like he was asleep, but Derrick saw his eyes move every now and then and figured he was just faking it, probably thinking about Derrick's stupid plan.

It had sounded great in the dark. The kidnapper couldn't watch them every second. He had to go to the bathroom and when he did, they'd raise one of the windows, kick out the screen and make a run for it.

They were fast. Derrick had won the relay race at school field day last year, and David had come in second. The kidnapper wouldn't have a chance to catch them if they had a head start. Sure, they might get lost in the woods, but Derrick wasn't worried about that. Uncle Matt had taken them camping lots of times and taught them all about survival. They'd find their way back to the road and wave down a passing car. Super easy.

Problem was that while they were locked in the bedroom last night, the kidnapper had nailed wood over the rest of the windows. That had made Derrick really mad, but he wasn't giving up. He just needed a better plan. He'd seen all the *Home Alone* movies a bunch of times. If that kid could take care of himself, so could Derrick and David.

In fact he and David could do it better. There were two of them and only one jerky kidnapper. That's why he wasn't really all that afraid. He'd let them out of the bedroom this morning, but the house was sealed tight. The kidnapper had the key to the front door and the back door was nailed shut.

The guy was lying on the lumpy old sofa now, whistling that same weird tune he was always whistling and watching a movie on the old TV that kept fading in and out. It looked like it could be a hundred years old, except their neighbor Billy Mack had told him they didn't have television back then.

Derrick waited for the commercial. The guy always hollered for him to shut up if he talked during the show. An advertisement for Dodge trucks popped up on the screen.

"How come you live out here all by yourself?"

"'Cause I'm not filthy rich like your parents."

"You could get a job and make some money."

"Don't get smart with me, kid."

"I wasn't."

The picture on the screen started rolling, and the man went over to fiddle with the knobs again. When that didn't work, he took the screwdriver from his back pocket and made a few adjustments on the back of the set. The picture steadied. He went back to the sofa and dropped the screwdriver onto the table next to him, beneath a heavy lamp that had scratch marks all over it.

Derrick walked over and propped on the edge of the sofa. He picked up the screwdriver and ran his fingers along the tapered tip. "Did you kidnap us 'cause our daddy's a superstar?"

"Who told you he was a superstar?"

"Nobody, but he is. He's been to the Pro Bowl three times."

"Is that what it takes these days for a kid to like his old man? You gotta be a superstar?"

"No," Derrick said. "You just have to love your kids like you're supposed to. Didn't your daddy love you?"

"Yeah. So much he beat me every time he got drunk and yelled at me when he was sober. Now, shut up. My show's back on."

"What about your mom?" Derrick asked, ignoring the man's comments to shut up.

"What about her?"

"Did she take care of you?"

"Yeah, sure, sometimes. When she was around. Enough with the questions. I didn't need nobody when I was a kid and don't need nobody now."

"Then why don't you just let us go?"

The guy didn't answer. But Derrick knew he wasn't going to let them go until he had the money from their parents, and he didn't see how Momma and Daddy would get five million dollars.

Derrick got up and walked to the kitchen though there was nothing in there to eat. They'd finished off the last two burgers for breakfast this morning. That had been hours ago. He wondered what Juanita was cooking for lunch.

He opened the refrigerator and looked at the empty shelves. That's when he heard the yell, a high-pitched shriek that sounded as if someone had their arm torn off at the shoulder. Derrick took off for the living room and then stopped in the doorway staring at the blood pooling on the floor by the couch.

Now he was scared.

"Quick, grab the door key out of his pocket, and get your jacket. We gotta get out of here," David yelled.

Derrick didn't move. He just stared at the kidnapper. The man was sprawled out on the floor behind the television set, blood pouring from a cut on the back of his head. The lamp was lying on the floor next to him, its shade at a cockeyed angle. "What happened?"

"He was tinkering with the TV, and I snuck up on him and hit him with the lamp."

"Do you think he's dead?"

"I don't know. C'mon. We have to get out of here now."

Derrick leaned over the man. He'd seen a dead cow before, but he'd never seen a dead man. It creeped him out, but he reached into the front pocket of the man's trousers and retrieved his key ring.

Derrick wasn't sure which one opened the door, so he tossed the key ring to David. He still wasn't sure if the man was breathing, but he could hear his own heart. It sounded like a banging drum.

David had found the right key and had the door open when Derrick saw the man's hand move. He wasn't dead, just knocked out. And when he came to, he was going to be roaring mad. Time to haul it.

Derrick picked up the screwdriver and grabbed his jacket from the back of a chair. He didn't know why he needed the tool, but it seemed like a good idea to have it. He took off running as fast as he could, finally catching up with David at the edge of the woods. They kept running, tripping over roots and getting hung up in branches and vines.

Derrick's legs started to ache. His chest hurt, too.

And he was thirsty. He was glad when David stopped and leaned against a tree trunk.

"Do you think he's chasing us?" Derrick asked when he'd caught his breath enough to talk.

"He thinks he's getting five million dollars for us," David said. "What do you think?"

"Yeah, but you hurt him bad."

"Nah. I knocked him out, but his legs will still work when he comes to. We have to keep moving and try to find a road."

"We should have stolen his cell phone," Derrick said. "Then we could have called Momma or Daddy or 911."

"Yeah, but we didn't. So we gotta keep on the move. I don't want to spend the night in the woods."

"We can do it if we have to." Derrick tried to sound brave since he hadn't done much toward helping them escape. "We've slept under the stars before when we were camping with Uncle Matt."

"We had food then," David said. "And lanterns."

And Uncle Matt, though neither of them mentioned that now. Derrick jumped at a sound like cracking twigs in the distance. And then they heard the man's voice calling their names.

"Keep up with me," David called, and he was off again with Derrick right behind him. "I don't want to have to really hurt that man."

Chapter Five

The fragrant smell of pine filled the house, just as it had every day since last Saturday when Lenora's sons had helped her drape the mantel and staircase with the fresh cut greenery. Her much-handled nativity was carefully placed along the top of the piano where they always gathered to sing carols after church on Christmas Eve.

Randolph, Lenora's deceased husband, had spent hours in his workshop, first cutting out and then coating each of the nativity figures with lead-free paint for Langston's first Christmas. The set had been a favorite of all her children from the time they were toddlers and first heard the story of the birth of the baby Jesus. David and Derrick had spent their share of time moving the figures around and playing with the miniature sheep, cattle and camels as well.

The house was almost the way it had always been mere days before Christmas—except that it was shrouded in anxiety and the season's joviality was hushed by the burden of heavy hearts. Only Jaime was making a stab at normalcy. She was sitting on the floor by the hearth, tape, scissors and rolls of shiny Christmas wrap at her elbow.

Christmas in the Collingsworth family had never been a time for lavish spending. When her children had been growing up, Lenora and Randolph had insisted that the focus of the season be on love and sharing with those less fortunate.

It was a tradition that had stuck, and instead of rabid shopping that they could well afford, each member of the family always put a lot of thought and frequently a lot of time and effort into their gifts.

Lenora's treats for her family had been carefully selected and wrapped weeks ago, but today she couldn't remember anything she'd bought except the skateboards the boys had picked out and begged for on a recent Houston shopping trip.

The front door to the house opened, and Lenora hurried into the hallway. Hopefully this time it would be Becky and Nick returning with the ransom money and not some pushy reporter who'd managed to bypass the guards at the gate.

Earlier today, one had cut down part of the fence to get on the property. Jim Bob had spotted him and sent him packing quickly enough. Like Matt said, if all their wranglers were as dependable as Jim Bob, running the ranch would be play.

"The money's in hand," Nick called, holding up a large valise. "Now all we need is that phone call."

"Then you haven't heard from the abductor today?"

"Not a word," Becky said, the weight of the situation dragging her voice the way it pulled at her face and painted dark circles beneath her eyes.

"I'll fix you a plate," Lenora said. "Trish and Jaclyn made chicken pasta and a salad for lunch."

Becky shook her head. "None for me. We stopped for lunch in Houston."

"Which she ate two bites of," Nick said.

He was sick over the boys but obviously worried about Becky as well. He was a good man, cocky and fun loving and sometimes she thought he had a football for a heart, but her sons liked Nick and that said a lot about his character. Lenora had always been sure he and Becky would work out their differences and make their marriage work.

But Becky was stubborn, always had been, and once she made up her mind about something, she developed a severe case of tunnel vision that never let her see another side.

She was a loving mother, though, generous to a fault. And unlike Jaime, she was seemingly unaware of her beauty or the fact that men were instantly attracted to her, as much for her grace and intellect as her stunning looks.

But stubborn, nonetheless. She'd no doubt inherited that trait from her grandfather. Jeremiah was the most hardheaded man Lenora had ever seen in her life. She'd be hard pressed to explain why everyone loved him. They just did. So did she.

Lenora and Nick followed Becky into the den.

Becky stopped next to the stack of wrapped gifts. "What are you doing?"

Jaime stuck a large red bow to a package. "Wrapping presents."

"How can you?" Becky's voice shook with unchecked emotion. "How can you go on like nothing's wrong when David and Derrick are in the hands of some madman?"

Jaime pulled a strip of tape from the dispenser. "Because I won't let myself believe that they're not going to walk though that door tonight with you and Nick, safe and excited to be home. When they do, they'll expect presents to shake and try to guess what's inside."

"But what if you're wrong? What if they don't come home tonight? What if…" Becky exploded, kicking one of the presents. It skidded across the thick rug and onto the wooden floor before thudding against the wall.

Jaime jumped up, dropping the roll of ribbon she'd just picked up as she pulled her sister into her arms. "Oh, Becky, you have to have faith that the boys are safe. We all do. We *have* to believe."

Both sisters were in tears now, holding on to each other while the fire crackled in the huge stone fireplace and streams of red satin entangled their feet. Tears burned at the back of Lenora's eyes. Jaime never ceased to amaze her. She'd never loved either daughter more.

NICK BACKED out of the den and went to the kitchen to get a cup of coffee though he was already so jumpy he could barely sit in one place for over five minutes. That and the ache in his neck and shoulders had made the ride back to the ranch pure torture.

There was a plate of homemade peanut butter cookies next to the coffeepot. There were always homemade cookies at Jack's Bluff. Juanita kept the freezer stuffed with them.

He picked up one. Still warm. One of his sisters-in-law must have done the baking honors in Juanita's absence. Everyone wanted to help. Everyone needed to keep busy.

He'd married into one terrific family—and then he'd blown it. How had he ever let things between him and Becky get to this point?

Who was he fooling? He'd known from the very beginning he wasn't the man Becky thought he was. She'd seen in him what she wanted to see, loved a man who hadn't really existed. It had just been a matter of time before she saw him for the fake he really was.

If anything, he'd loved Becky too much. He still did. There wasn't a day he didn't miss having her in his life, not a night that he didn't long to have her in his bed and in his arms. He couldn't even imagine making love to another woman.

But he'd never expected to bring this kind of terror into all their lives. If he hadn't gotten hurt... If they hadn't shown the boys' picture on TV... If the boys hadn't had to go to school Monday to make up for those lost hurricane days instead of already being out for the holidays...

So many ifs, but the biggest one now was if he was doing the right thing in not going to the police or trying to bring the FBI in on this. He wanted to believe he was right, but the longer this took, the more the doubts tormented him. What if he was wrong and the man never called back?

He put the cookie to his lips, then pulled his hand away and dropped the morsel into the trash. His stomach was still struggling to digest the ham sandwich he'd forced down at lunch. He was filling a pottery mug with the strong coffee when his cell phone jangled.

The coffee spilled over his fingers as he set the cup down, stuck his hand into his pocket and gripped the phone. He answered without bothering to check the caller ID. "Hello."

"This is Dr. Cambridge's nurse. I'm calling for Nick Ridgely."

Damn. The doctor's office. They'd badger him about getting back to the hospital so that they could finish the tests. The head trainer for the team had already called him about the same thing twice today. He didn't have time for this.

"This is Nick Ridgely, but I'm expecting a very important call and can't tie up my phone right now."

"This is an important call, Mr. Ridgely. The doctor needs to speak with you. Hold on. He's right here."

The seconds Nick waited seemed interminable. His phone line needed to remain open.

"We didn't meet, but I'm one of the staff neurosurgeons at the hospital where you were treated Sunday night. My colleague Dr. Krause asked me to review your records."

"I understand, but I can't talk now. I'll have to call you back later."

The doctor kept talking. "You left the hospital in a hurry."

"There was a family emergency. I signed the AMA form."

"I understand that. Are you still in a lot of pain?"

"Some." To put it mildly. To put it more accurately, the pain was constant, but waiting for a call from the abductor was a thousand times worse.

"I can't stress enough how important it is for you to check back in the hospital, Mr. Ridgely. It's urgent that we get a CAT scan and an MRI."

"Yeah, right. I'll do that one day next week."

"I don't think you understand the seriousness or potential damage you may suffer from your injury."

"Okay, give it to me straight—and fast. What's the worse that can happen?"

"The X-rays indicate that you may have a unilateral locked facet. It's not a common injury even in football, but it happens when the neck is flexed and rotated at the same time. The risk is that the spine may be unstable and can slip. Any sudden movement or bending of your neck could leave you paralyzed."

Nick fought the urge to slam a fist into the wall. He couldn't deal with this now. He had a contusion or whatever the hell the E.R. doc had said the other night. He just needed time for it to heal and he'd be fine. If it was something worse, he'd surely know it.

"Thanks for calling, Dr. Cambridge. I'll come back in for the tests as soon as I can."

It wasn't until the conversation was over and the connection broken that he realized Becky was standing in the doorway to the kitchen watching him. He had no idea how much of the conversation she'd heard.

"What's wrong?" she asked.

He shook his head. "Nothing." He needed to play this cool for her sake, though he felt anything but.

"Who was on the phone?"

"Dr. Cambridge reminding me that he needs to check out my neck in a few days."

"That's all?"

"That's it."

"You're lying, Nick. I heard the apprehension in your voice when you were on the phone, and it's written all over your face now."

"It's no big deal, Becky. I may miss a game or two." He turned his back on her and stamped toward the back door, not bothering to grab a jacket. Had it been freezing he doubted he'd feel the cold. How could he when he was sinking into hell?

Paralysis. A devil of a diagnosis to hold over a man whose sons were in danger. It wasn't like he could just walk away from the kidnapping. He'd be careful. No sudden moves. That was the best he could do.

NICK HAD SHUT her out again, just like always. Becky had seen his face when he was talking to the doctor. The news had been bad, but instead of sharing with her, he'd stalked out the back door to deal with his problems without her.

It shouldn't matter so much in light of all that was going on. It shouldn't but it did, maybe because of what they were going through.

He expected her to lean on him, but he was not about to let himself need any emotional support from her. Not about to admit that he was upset over some damn football injury that he admitted wasn't serious.

Maybe he found it easier to confide in Brianna.

Anger and bitterness pooled in Becky's stomach until she stormed out the back door and down the steps. When she spotted Nick walking toward the stables, she ran to catch up with him. He turned, saw that it was her footfalls he'd heard and kept walking.

He didn't stop until he reached the railed fence that surrounded the riding arena. He propped his elbows on the top rung and stared straight ahead as if there were something to see.

A gust of wind cut through Becky's thin cotton shirt, and she hugged her arms around her chest as she approached him. Her nerves were raw, her composure diminished to the point she had to hold on to the railing to keep steady. "What was that about?"

"I don't know what you're talking about."

"Your rushing off to brood over your injury instead of telling me what the doctor said."

"I'm not brooding."

"I think you are. All that talk of being here for Christmas with the boys was just your guilt talking, wasn't it? Well, if you think I'm worried about your career while my boys are missing, you're dead wrong."

"The thought never entered my mind. But just for the record, do you actually think I'm *not* going through hell every second David and Derrick are with that lunatic?"

"I don't know what you're feeling, Nick, but whatever it is, I'm sure football and your star performance is involved in it."

She stepped away, realizing she said too much. She let her temper and vulnerability get the better of her.

Nick grabbed her arm and held her, his gaze so intense his dark eyes seemed to be searing into hers. "I won't contest the divorce any longer, Becky. I'll sign whatever you say."

She shivered as he kicked at a clod of dirt before releasing her and walking away. The finality of their relationship had never felt so real. But it was what she wanted. Holding on to a corpse wouldn't bring it back to life.

The analogy sent new chills up her spine to eventually settle deep in her bones. She forced herself to follow Nick back to the house.

The boys' safety was all that mattered, and Nick and his cell phone were her one link to her sons. No matter how she and Nick felt about each other, they had to get through this together.

BULL MUTTERED a new series of curses with every step he made in the growing darkness. His head felt as if it were splitting open and his brains were draining into the huge knot that had formed around the cut on the back of his head.

The blood had matted in his hair, and when he touched the wound, it felt like the sticky mess that had passed for oatmeal in the penitentiary. It gagged him, and he'd thrown up once, though the nausea was probably more from the throbbing pain at the base of his skull than the repulsive feel of his bloody scalp.

He'd never expected Nick's sons would go violent on him. They had to get their nasty streak from their father. Big-shot NFL receiver. No wonder Becky had separated from him.

He stopped and leaned against a tree trunk, gasping for air and trying to get his bearings before he was the one lost in these stinking woods. The image of Becky fixed in his murky mind until he dissolved into a fit of coughing.

He had to find those boys. Nick would never pay off if he couldn't produce them. No money. No flight to Mexico.

Worse, if the kids got free, they'd be able to identify him and he'd end up back in prison. No way he could let that happen. He had to find the vicious little devils before they reached the highway and flagged down a passing motorist.

Just his luck they'd been too smart to head back down the dirt road near the cabin to the highway. If they had, he could have taken his car and easily caught them before they reached help.

But the prints of their tennis shoes had led straight into the woods. He'd been able to track them easily at first, before they'd reached higher, dryer ground. Half the time they'd wandered in larger and larger circles—which meant they couldn't be that far away now.

But it was getting darker, and he'd lost all sight of their trail a good half hour ago.

An owl hooted overhead, claiming his hunting grounds for the night. Well, the dumb bird would have to share it. Something slithered at his feet. It was too cold for snakes to be slinking though the pine straw, but still he tensed as he searched the ground.

He didn't see the escaping creature, but he saw something a whole lot better. A screwdriver. He picked it up and rolled the amber handle around in his hand. It was his, all right, at least it was the one he used to constantly tinker with that piece-of-crap TV.

Apparently the boys had taken it with them when they'd gone on the run. Which meant they'd been in this exact spot, likely minutes ago. His heart began to pound, bringing more pain but still urging him on. It was almost as if he could smell the boys now.

This time when he got them in hand, there would be no more Mr. Nice Guy. He wouldn't be made a fool of twice.

The twenty-four hours were up. Nick would be waiting for his call. He might be the rich, NFL superstar, but there wouldn't be one damn thing he could do but wait.

Besting Nick Ridgely was almost as good a prize as the cash.

Chapter Six

The twenty-four hour mark came and went with no word from the abductor. By eight-thirty Tuesday night, Becky felt as if every breath took supreme effort and every heartbeat pumped new agony into her veins. Earlier the family den in the big house had been crackling with anticipation and conversation.

Even then every phrase and syllable had sounded forced, brave attempts to keep the mood positive. The family was all still present, but the silence now was like an icy spray that froze the oxygen in the still, heavy air.

They'd done everything the abductor had asked. The ransom was waiting. The plane was ready to go. Langston was planning to fly the plane himself, and Zach would go along as copilot.

But with each tick of the clock, the dread swelled. So did the doubts.

Following Nick's wishes to leave the cops out of this might have been a monumental mistake. Had they put out an instant AMBER Alert, the boys might be home tonight, sleeping in their own beds. No one was blaming him, but she was certain he was second-guessing himself though they'd barely spoken since her blow up this afternoon.

Nick walked to the hearth and propped both hands on the mantel, leaning close even though the earlier blaze had died to glowing embers. His face was drawn, his neck corded from muscles that looked taut enough to break.

Zach walked over to stand beside him. Blackie padded over to Becky and cocked his head to the side; the lab's dark, soulful eyes peered into hers. She patted his head absently, sure that he not only missed his masters but sensed the tension.

Zach put a hand on Nick's shoulder. "I can get the ball rolling with police involvement anytime you say. All you have to do is give me the word."

Nick nodded.

"Another option might be to hire a team of private investigators," Matt said.

"Or we could get a search party organized," Bart added. "There's not a man in the county who wouldn't be out there right now going door to door to see if anyone's seen David and Derrick or knows anything about the abduction."

"And then the media circus would take over," Langston said. "But maybe that would help flush this guy out. I just don't know."

"That's the problem," Nick said. "There's no way to know."

"Why doesn't he call?" Becky lamented out loud, saying what they all were thinking. "If he wants the money, why doesn't he call?" The terror tore at her throat and her voice.

Jaime came over and settled on the arm of her chair, slipping an arm around Becky's shoulders. "He's going to call, sis. He may be rethinking the exchange, but he's going to call."

"You don't know that. Those are just empty words."

Trish walked in with a plate of oatmeal cookies and a bowl of sliced apples. She set them on the coffee table and slid onto the sofa beside Langston.

"Becky and I have to talk," Nick said.

"We'll clear out," Jaime said, "and give you a little privacy."

"No." Becky stood and struggled for a grip on her composure. "All of you stay as long as you want. I need some fresh air. Nick and I can take a walk."

Nick nodded again. "I'm not discounting any of your advice, guys. And I'll tell you this, I don't know of a single person on earth I'd rather have in this with me than the Collingsworth clan. That includes the FBI or any police force in the world."

"But don't rule any of that out," Langston reminded him. "It's not either/or. You can have us and professionals."

Becky paused to give her mother's hand a squeeze as she passed her. "Keep praying," she whispered.

"Always."

This time Becky stopped for a jacket and took a flashlight from the rack by the back door. She didn't wait for Nick, but she heard the crinkle of leather as he pulled on his own jacket and followed her.

She noticed everything, the creaking of the top step when she put her foot on it, the rustle of the wind in the oak trees, the sting of cold air on her cheeks.

It was as if the totality of her being had been crammed into this moment and the decisions they were about to make. Her boys' safe return, their very lives might depend on what she and Nick did in the next few minutes and the next few hours. She wouldn't leave this all to him the way she had earlier.

Nick caught up with her hurried stride and fell in beside her. "I thought we'd hear from the abductor by now. I was sure he just wanted his hands on the money as soon as possible."

"And now you've changed your mind?" she asked, fighting her frustration.

"Not entirely. There's no reason for him not to call us if it's the ransom he wants. He may have met with complications."

"How complicated can it be to make a phone call?"

"He could be driving somewhere to use a public phone or to buy one with limited minutes from the convenience store. He'll want to make sure we can't use the phone to find him before he's ready to close the deal. Maybe he got caught in traffic."

"You think he's just driving around with our boys in the car? How is he keeping them quiet? He might have them drugged them or locked up in the trunk. Maybe that's why he said they weren't available the first time he called."

Her voice climbed steadily higher. Worse, she wasn't even sure she was making sense, but terrifying possibilities were storming her mind.

"Maybe he's just enjoying his power to keep us on edge," he countered.

"More than he'd enjoy five million dollars in his

hand?" No. If this were only about the money, he would have called. They could have delivered it to him tonight. He could be in Mexico. This could all be over.

"We can't just sit here and do nothing, Nick. He might be taking the boys out of the country or taking them who knows where. The longer we wait, the more difficult it will be to track him down. And…"

The rest of the sentence was swallowed by the growing lump in her throat. Nick put a hand on her shoulder. Her chest constricted painfully at his touch. She needed his strength, needed him. Yet she couldn't let herself lean on him. Reluctantly, she pulled away.

"Does my touch bother you that much, Becky?"

Yes, in ways she couldn't deal with in this situation. "I'm just trying to get through this, Nick. I have to be strong."

"We're in this together."

"I can't very well ignore that, can I, Nick, since you're the one the abductor contacts—or doesn't contact. You're the one making the decisions." The bitterness crept into her voice. She wished it hadn't, but there was too much at risk here to worry about that now.

Nick's cell phone rang. Becky's heart jumped to her throat. Please let it be the abductor. *Please let him be ready to give her back her sons.*

Nick's hello was firm, in control. She held her breath then released a sharp, painful exhale when she heard the agitation in Nick's voice.

Something was wrong. Her legs went weak, but somehow she kept standing, her mind grasping for meaning in every word Nick spoke.

"HELLO, NICKY BOY. I guess you realize by now that there's been a slight delay in our plans."

The cocky bastard. He was enjoying their torment. Nick's teeth ground together and his muscles clenched. "You said five million in small bills and a flight out of the country. I'm ready to meet those demands, so let's get this over and done with."

"Not so fast, champ. The boys are asleep. You don't want me dragging them out in the middle of the night, do you? Besides, I have a couple of things I need to take care of before I tell America *adios.*"

"I want my boys, and I want them now. Tell me where to meet you or I go to the cops."

"That would be a major mistake if you want to get them back alive."

"Let me talk to them."

"I told you they're sleeping. I'll have them call you in the morning. We'll talk specifics then. But there is one other thing. I've decided I need a hostage with me on the flight to Mexico. You know, someone to be sure you don't plan any tricks like aborting the flight once you have your sons. I'm thinking having Becky along would be a great insurance plan."

Nick's body went rigid. "My wife is not a bargaining tool."

"Why not? You've already replaced her with Brianna Campbell. You're surely not so selfish as to deny me the pleasure of her company on a short flight."

"Five million. Do you want it or not?"

"You do realize that you're not calling the shots here, Nick. I want Becky on that plane. If there's any funny stuff, she takes a bullet. That way I know you won't have an armed greeting party waiting for me when we land."

"You want a hostage, you can have me. That's my best offer."

"I'll sleep on it and let you know in the morning."

"Let me talk to the boys." The menacing click of the phone as it disconnected swallowed his demand. Nick stood still, his back ramrod straight, numb to the pain from his injury.

"What's wrong?" Becky demanded.

"Change in plans," he said.

"What kind of change?"

"Let's go to the porch. I talk better when I'm sitting." And he needed a minute to digest the kidnapper's new demand. Not that he'd even consider letting Becky get on a plane with that lunatic, even if she agreed. Their divorce wasn't final yet. She was still his wife and the mother of his sons.

She was still his to protect.

A LITTLE MORE than a half hour later, Nick and Becky sat down at the big oak table in the dining room with the core members of the Collingsworth family around them. The somber mood was foreign to the familiar setting where Nick had joined in many family celebrations and marvelous Sunday brunches.

The room was virtually unchanged from the way it had looked the Sunday morning he and Becky had officially announced their engagement, though it had been almost totally destroyed in the explosion this past summer.

That day the entire family had almost lost their lives for the sin of befriending and trusting the wrong man.

Had it not been for the quick thinking of Matt's wife, Shelly, they would have been obliterated, his sons along with them.

If there was any weakness in the Collingsworths, it was their willingness to see the best in people. They'd certainly done that with Nick. Tonight that trust felt like weights pressing into his chest. He'd insisted on laying out the game plan, on going with his instincts. He'd made critical mistakes.

He'd failed the people who needed him most. Not for the first time and the memories that admittance unleashed were attacking him full force.

Langston took the seat at the head of the table. Lenora sat at the other end. Becky sat between him and Zach on one side of the table. Jaime, Bart, Matt and his wife, Shelly, sat opposite them. Jeremiah was still keeping to his room and had not been apprised of the situation. Had the elderly gentleman with the temper of Attila the Hun and the determination of a bull known, Nick was certain he'd have been right there with them.

Becky had specifically requested Shelly's presence. Her CIA experience might be invaluable. The other wives had suggested they not be part of the decision-making process though they were there to help in any way they could. The solidarity of the Collingsworths in crisis was nothing short of astonishing.

Nick was fairly certain the room had never been this quiet before. It was as if all of them were holding their collective breaths waiting to hear what Becky had to say. She'd held up so well on the porch that Nick had feared she was slipping into shock.

That wasn't the case. She was stronger than he'd

ever known. Courageous. Determined. And ready to
fight. She was a hell of a woman. Always had been.
Maybe her strength had been their downfall, though it
was definitely helping to hold him together now.

Nick filled the family in with the basics of his latest
conversation with the abductor, minus the information
about his wanting Becky for a hostage. He hadn't even
mentioned that to her. It wasn't an option, so there was
no reason to bring it up for discussion.

The family listened without interrupting until he was
through, but he could sense the dread imbedding more
deeply in their souls as he talked.

"I obviously misjudged the situation," Nick said. "I
should have listened to the rest of you in the first place."

"Not necessarily," Shelly offered, the tone of her
voice indicating the observation was more than sym-
pathy. "You sensed the man was desperate and acting
on impulse after seeing the boys' picture on the news.
First instincts are frequently right on target. But that
same impulsiveness might also make him edgy after the
fact, and he may fear he's walking into a trap, thus his
hesitance to make the exchange."

"But wouldn't his being on the edge make him even
more dangerous?" Jaime asked. "Wouldn't that be more
reason to move on this quickly and with every weapon
in the arsenal?"

Shelly nodded. "Especially since we can't accurately judge the man's mental condition. But at the
same time, we don't want to do anything to cause him
to hurt the boys."

"Which is what might happen if we let the media get

hold of this," Becky said. "Nick and I have talked and made the decision that we can't take that risk."

"So what are you saying?" Zach asked. "That you don't want police involvement? If so, I think you're making a big mistake."

"No, we just want to keep this as quiet as possible. We're open to suggestions."

Zach nodded. "At the very least, we need an APB out to all the law enforcement officers in at least a three-state area to be on the lookout for David and Derrick. And we need to contact the border patrol."

"I'd say that's top priority," Matt said. "We can't let him take the boys into Mexico."

They were talking prevention, but for all they knew, the man could have crossed that border with David and Derrick hours ago. That, too, would be Nick's fault. No one said it, but they all knew it.

"With that much law enforcement involved, word of the abduction is going to leak to the media," Langston said.

"Not necessarily," Zach said. "At least not before we can track the boys down. Everyone takes crime involving kids seriously. Besides, I think it's a risk we have to take."

"And we need a description of that car that Eddie Mason saw them getting into," Lenora said.

"I've got you covered there," Zach said.

"Black Oldsmobile sedan. An old one, an eighties model he thought. Dent in back right fender with patch of rust showing through. No hubcaps."

"When did you talk to Eddie Mason?" Nick asked. "I thought we'd agreed you wouldn't."

"I didn't. There are more subtle ways to get information. I just mentioned to the crossing guard that someone had reported seeing a group of teenagers speeding though the area on Monday about the time school let out and asked if he'd seen it. When he said no, I asked if he'd noticed any unfamiliar cars in the area."

"Did he say he saw David and Derrick get into the Oldsmobile?"

"No, but he said the car had driven by the school a few times before the closing bell. That made him suspicious, and he was about to call in a report to the sheriff's department when the bell rang and the kids came pouring out."

"Then we don't know if that's the same car," Matt said.

"We wouldn't if he'd left it at that, but when I asked if he'd seen the car again, he said that when he got a break from the crossing duties he spotted the same car parked across the street from the church.

"Two boys climbed in and the driver pulled away, so he figured it was just a relative who didn't know the rule about where to pick up students."

"Did he say anything about the driver?"

"That he wasn't a teenager and he wasn't speeding, since he thought that's what I was investigating. Said the driver looked to be in his late twenties, maybe older, but he'd just gotten a glimpse of him."

"Thanks," Nick said. "At least we have that much to go on."

"I'd still like to call my contact at the FBI," Langston said, "and get his take on this."

"I agree," Shelly said.

"And so do Nick and I," Becky said. "We've made that decision."

Becky had suggested it first, and Nick had been in total agreement. He'd forced himself to believe things would never get this far, that if he followed the abductor's orders to the letter his boys would be home tonight. Now the terrifying possibilities he'd worked so hard to keep at bay filled his mind.

It had to be the same for Becky. He ached to reach out to her in spite of their run-in this afternoon, but he couldn't face a rebuff right now. This was all so damn hard, their years together counting for nothing.

Nick took a deep breath and exhaled slowly. They were passing the point of no return as far as following the abductor's orders, but he couldn't stall any longer. "Call your friend at the bureau, Langston."

"You've got it." Langston stood and left the room to make the call without waiting for the rest of the decisions to be made.

"What about Zach?" Bart asked. "What do you want him to do? I'd put as much faith in him as I would the bureau—not that I don't think you should use them, too."

"Let's see what Langston finds out and then decide about that," Nick said.

"What if he's already crossed the border into Mexico? Then what?"

A choking knot clogged Nick's throat when he saw the fright in Becky's haunted eyes.

"Alert the border patrol to be on the watch for the car and them," Nick said. "See if we need to hire our own people to make sure he doesn't get that far. Do whatever it takes."

"In the meantime, I'm taking a drive and looking for

an old rusted, dented, navy Oldsmobile," Matt said. "Sitting here doing nothing is maddening."

"I'm with you," Bart said.

"I'll stick to my prayers," Lenora said. She walked over and put her arm around Becky. "You need some rest, sweetheart."

"I can't sleep, Mother."

"Then just come and lie down in my room for awhile. Exhaustion won't help the boys or your decision-making abilities."

Jaime and Shelly left with them, leaving only Nick and Zach at the table.

Zach stood and walked to the window, staring into the darkness before turning back to Nick. "Are you sure you've told us everything?"

Nick hesitated, but he knew he could trust Zach. "The kidnapper wants to take Becky as hostage when Langston flies him to Mexico."

"That's interesting."

"Don't tell me you think that's a good idea."

"No, absolutely not. I just wonder if it's possible he knows Becky."

Nick trailed his fingers up and down his neck, keeping the pressure light. "What are you getting at?"

"Just that if he knows Becky, that would narrow the suspects down considerably."

"I'm not sure how. Half the people in Houston know Becky or at least know of her. The Collingsworths are too active in local charities and arts foundations for them not to have heard of her."

"Yes, but half the people in America know who you are."

"Good point. He did call Becky by name, but that doesn't really prove he's had contact with her."

"Are you sure he didn't say anything that might give us a hint as to where he is?"

"No."

"Does he have a Texas accent?"

"Definitely."

"How was the grammar?"

"I don't see how this is helping."

"It could give us an idea of his background."

"His language is rough around the edges. Some slang. Nothing particularly unusual."

"I hate to even bring this up, but I've checked the files of all the registered people guilty of sex crimes living in this and neighboring counties. There aren't many in our immediate area, and I've made routine calls on all of them without giving any indication that I was investigating a crime. None of them have the boys with them. Of course that doesn't guarantee they aren't involved."

"Thanks, Zach. I really appreciate your efforts."

"The boys may be my nephews, but I don't think I could love them more if they were my own. They're great kids."

"Yeah." They were Nick's own, yet Zach had probably seen more of them this last year than he had. That said a lot for his quality of fatherhood, a point that Becky had been stressing for years.

Zach walked over to Nick and delivered a manly punch to the forearm. "I know this is tough, but hang in there, buddy. The boys are counting on you."

Langston stepped back into the doorway. "The FBI

is sending out an agent from Houston who specializes in abductions. He'll be here in a matter of hours. Nick and Becky should probably try to get some sleep in the meantime."

"Fast work," Zach commented. "Pays to have friends in high places."

"Pays to have friends period," Langston said.

And it paid to have the clout of the Collingsworths on your side. Nick had to hold on to the faith that it and Lenora's prayers would be enough.

"LOOK," DAVID SAID.

"At what?" Derrick stumbled though the brush, hurrying to catch up with his twin brother. He was tired of walking. They should have come to a road hours ago. He wished he had his compass or that he'd paid more attention when Uncle Zach had been teaching him about using the stars to find your way home if you got lost in the woods.

"Look, through those trees. Somebody must live there."

"Oh, man! Am I glad to see that!" He was beginning to think they were going to be stuck out here all night—or until the kidnapper found them, which would be a lot worse.

They kept walking until they got a better look at the place. "Do you think somebody lives there?" David asked. "I don't see any cars around."

"It looks kind of empty, all right. But if there's a mobile home there has to be a road for people to get here. We can follow it to the highway."

"Yeah, and if someone lives there but isn't home, there still might be food."

"And water," Derrick added. "I'm really thirsty."

"Let's check it out."

"Maybe they have a phone, and we can call Mom to come get us."

"Now, that's what I'm talking about." David took off at a dead run toward the mobile home with Derrick on his heels. Before he got there, he slid to a stop, grabbing Derrick's arm and almost making him fall.

"What's wrong?" Derrick asked.

"Suppose the kidnapper is in there waiting for us?"

"Why would he be? He didn't know we'd come this way."

"Still, he just might be in there. Or a friend of his might live there."

"We'll peek through the window before we go inside," Derrick said. He led the way, marching as if they were soldiers. When he got closer to the house, he sneaked to the side and rose up to the tips of his toes so he could see inside the window.

"Well?" David whispered.

"Gimme a minute. It's dark in there." But there was a stream of moonlight lighting the area right in front of the window. Derrick didn't see anybody, and the place was quiet.

"I think it's all clear," he said, still keeping his voice low just in case. "Let's grab a broken limb for a weapon, but I don't think we'll need it. If the kidnapper were here, he would have left the light on to lure us in. And if somebody else is here, they'll help us get home."

They grabbed the sticks and climbed the three steps to a porch so small it wouldn't have held them and Blackie.

David knocked. Nobody answered. "Hey, anybody in there?" Still no response. He tried the knob. "It's locked."

Derrick propped his weapon against the house. "Then I guess we'll have to break in."

"We could go to jail for that."

Derrick shook his head. "Naw. We've escaped from a kidnapper. They'll just be talking about how brave we are."

"How do we get in?"

"We can break out a window."

"I was just about to say that," David said.

"Sure you were."

"I was, 'cause see that big rock out by the road. We can hurl it through the glass."

"But you better let me throw it," Derrick said, "'cause I can chuck it harder than you can." He wasn't sure that was right, but if they got into trouble for breaking out the window, he should face it since he suggested they break in.

David got the rock and handed it to him. He threw it as hard as he could. The rock went right through the pane, and glass shattered and scattered all over the ground.

"I'll heft you up to my shoulders," Derrick said. "You can reach in and unlock the window."

David took off his jacket and wrapped it around his right hand and arm so he wouldn't get cut. David was good at thinking of stuff like that. Once he was on Derrick's shoulders, he knocked out the rest of the window and just climbed through. "I'll unlock the door for you," he called, then disappeared into the dark house.

By the time Derrick got back around to the front door, it was standing open and the lights were on. The mobile home smelled like wet, dirty socks but it had furniture. Old stuff.

"Let's check out the kitchen," David said.

Derrick was right behind him. The refrigerator was mostly empty except for a few slices of cheese. There were a bunch of bottles of water though. Derrick took one for himself and handed one to David. He swallowed half of his in one gulp.

"There's sodas, too," he said. He opened the door to the freezer. There were bunches of packages of meat. "Ice cream sandwiches," he said, pulling out the box of frozen treats.

David crawled up on the countertop to reach the higher shelves. "Not much in here but canned stuff. Chili. Chicken noodle soup." He shoved the cans around to reach to the back of the shelf. "And two cans of spaghetti with franks like Dad made one time at his house. All we need is a can opener and a pan to warm it."

"Now you're talking." This was starting to feel like an adventure. "Spaghetti and ice-cream sandwiches for dessert?" Derrick took another long swig of his water as he opened another cabinet. "I found a pan."

"Yeah, I was so hungry I almost forgot about that. David jumped down from the counter. "But I think I'll have dessert first." He grabbed an ice cream sandwich and took off to search for the phone.

They both had dessert first, but David didn't find a phone. Derrick was still plenty hungry when the canned pasta and sauce was ready. They divided it up into two big bowls and took them to the small table.

"Tastes just like Dad's," David said.

"Yeah, but not as good as Grandma's or Juanita's."

"You think Blackie misses us?"

"Yeah," Derrick said. "I wish he was here. We could sic him on the kidnapper."

"We don't need that. We got away all by ourselves. I think my screwdriver idea fooled him into going the wrong way to look for us after we took off our shoes and walked in the creek so he'd lose our tracks."

"Yeah, but that water was really cold." Derrick finished his food. He'd planned to eat another ice cream sandwich, but he was too full. He might have a soda, though. He spied a rope on a nail on the wall. He walked over, picked it up and tied a slipknot like he did when he practiced calf roping. "Do you think we should sleep here tonight?"

"I don't think so. The kidnapper might show up and grab us in our sleep. We better keep walking and try to reach a highway. We could follow that road outside but stay in the woods in case the kidnapper comes driving down it looking for us."

"I hope we get home in time for the Christmas pageant," Derrick said. "We could tell everybody how we escaped."

"The girls will think we're superheroes."

"Cool."

Derrick swung the rope, lassoing the back of an empty chair. "We should probably get going. The ice cream would melt if we tried to take it with us, but we can take some soda and water in our jacket pockets. I think I'll take the rope, too."

He put his jacket back on, rolled the rope and tucked

it away in the big inside pocket. He stuffed the rest of his pockets with water. "I look fat," he said.

"Did you hear that?"

Derrick listened, and there it was. Whistling. The same stupid song the kidnapper always whistled. The adventure wasn't fun anymore.

Chapter Seven

The house was quiet, shrouded in a dismal dread that felt as if they'd been plucked from Jack's Bluff Ranch and dropped on a cold, dark planet. Lenora felt the desperation and ached for her dead husband the way she hadn't in a long, long time.

Not a day went by that she didn't miss him. Not the ferocious shredding of her heart kind of pain she had suffered the first months after his death. She couldn't have survived over two decades of that. Now it was a more a melancholy vacuum that even her marvelous family couldn't completely fill.

Lenora stood at the front door watching as the rear lights of Trish's car faded in the distance. She was taking Gina and her infant son, Randy, back to their cabin for the night so that the baby could sleep in his crib. Trish was a good mother and knew her baby and especially her teenage daughter needed a break from the fear and tension that saturated the big house.

Gina was taking this really hard, her usually high teenage spirits scraping the bottom. She'd spent most of the afternoon lying listless on the floor or out walking with Blackie. Lenora's granddaughter looked as woeful as the nine-month-old pup.

When Zach's wife, Kali, had gone back to their ranch to check on a new foal, she'd brought Blackie's brother Chideaux back to Jack's Bluff with her. In an emotional crunch, two loving dogs were always better than one, and both Lenora and Kali had insisted Gina take the dogs with her for the night.

Bart's wife, Jaclyn, had left with Trish. Nick had insisted she try to get a good night's sleep for the sake of their unborn daughter. The rest of the family was still inside, waiting. Endlessly waiting.

As if drawn into the darkness and the solitude of the Texas night, Lenora pushed out the front door, her footfalls sounding on the wooden planks of the porch. The night air was brisk but not cold. The temperature had climbed into the sixties this afternoon, not unusual for December in this part of Texas. The low tonight would only be in the upper forties.

Wherever the boys were, they would likely be warm enough. But were they safe? Did they have food? Were they afraid?

Lenora started toward the porch swing but then changed her direction, descending the steps instead. The noises and smells of the night wrapped around her like the arm of an old friend as she took the well-worn, moonlit path to the huge oak tree where she'd laid Randolph to rest so long ago.

She fell to her knees at the tombstone and rested her head against the smooth marker as salty tears pushed from her eyes.

"Oh, Randolph. I miss you so desperately. If you

were here, you'd take control. You'd know how to get our precious grandsons back." Her tears fell harder as her words shifted to a prayer.

"I trust you, God. I always have. I try not to ask for much, but I'm pleading with you to watch over David and Derrick. I'll bear anything you lay on me without complaining, but please bring my grandsons home safely."

Minutes later, the sobs and tears subsided and soothing warmth seeped inside her. She felt as if Randolph had reached from the grave and cradled her in his arms, giving her new hope.

She stayed at the grave site until her knees ached from being pressed into the grassy earth. She had no clear concept of how much time had passed before she started back toward the house.

She saw only the shadow outlined in the moonlight near the house, but she knew it was Becky. She hurried toward her, wondering if Becky had come looking for her, hoping it was with good news.

Becky looked up as Lenora approached. "Mom, what are you doing out here all by yourself?"

Odd to hear it put that way when she'd felt anything but alone. She walked over and clasped Becky's hand. "I went for a walk. Are you okay?"

"No. I'm afraid."

"I know, sweetheart. You're doing all you can. You have to trust God with the rest."

"I wish I had the faith you do, but I don't."

And more reassurances that the boys were going to be fine would sound trite and placating to Becky. "When you talked to the boys they sounded fine," she said, going for evidence Becky couldn't deny. "There's no reason to think that's changed."

"Then why didn't the kidnapper let us talk to them the last time he called? And why doesn't he call again?"

"I don't know. Maybe he can't get to a phone he trusts. Maybe he fell asleep."

"I should have never listened to Nick. I should have had an AMBER Alert go out right away. I should have called in the FBI sooner. Nick doesn't know anything about dealing with kidnappers."

The bitterness in her voice cut straight to Lenora's heart. "Don't be so hard on Nick, Becky. No one could have known the kidnapper wouldn't call as he said. Nick loves the boys. You know that."

"I suppose—in his way."

"That's the only way any of us can love—in our own way. You need Nick in this, Becky, and he needs you."

"Why would he need me? Haven't you heard? He has Brianna Campbell."

"I don't believe anything they print in those gossip magazines, certainly not that."

"It's more than gossip. She answered the phone when I called his hospital room after the accident."

Lenora swallowed hard. She had never given up on Becky and Nick getting back together, not even when the divorce papers were filed. They'd loved each other so much once. How could they throw their marriage away when they had two precious sons who needed them both?

Divorce was right for some people. She accepted that—but not for Becky and Nick.

The conversation was interrupted by the sound of a car engine and the illumination from the headlights of an approaching car. An unfamiliar black sedan pulled up in the drive and stopped a few feet from where they were standing. A lone man climbed out and started toward them.

The FBI had apparently arrived.

DERRICK TWISTED his hands and tried to loosen the duct tape that bound his wrists behind his back. No luck. His ankles were bound, too. Same with David. Worse, the goon had put David in the bedroom and left Derrick on the lumpy sofa so they couldn't even talk to each other.

He and David tried to run away when they'd heard that stupid whistling. They would have made it, too, if David hadn't tripped while running for the back door. Derrick had come back to help him, and that's when the man had grabbed both of them and put a killer grip around their necks with his muscular arms.

They'd tried to fight him off, but he was too strong for them. He'd locked David in the bathroom at the mobile home and dragged Derrick to the kitchen where he'd found the duct tape. Then he'd left them both tied up and locked in the bathroom while he'd gone back to his cabin for his grungy old car.

Now they were worse off than they'd been before they'd escaped. Derrick blamed himself for that. He should have been smart enough to just grab some food and water and clear out of that mobile home before the kidnapper had found them and brought them back to his cabin.

The kidnapper stomped on a giant roach crawling across the floor.

"I'm hungry," Derrick said. He wasn't, but he hoped

the abductor would leave them alone again and go after food. That would give him some time to come up with a better escape plan, one where they wouldn't get caught.

"You think I care if you brats starve? You're lucky I didn't beat you to death for attacking me and running off."

"You beat us and you'll be sorry. My daddy is probably going to kill you anyway."

"I'm not scared of your daddy or your rich uncles, either."

If that was true, the guy was dumber than he looked. The only problem was that neither his daddy nor his uncles knew where to find them.

"Cut out the yakking," the kidnapper said. "I'm going to call your parents, and when I get them on the line, you tell them I'm treating you well."

"Why would I tell them that when you got me and David tied up?"

"'Cause I'm telling you to. And because if you don't, I'll take this belt off and stripe your behinds with it the same way my daddy used to do to me."

"Really? Your dad did that?"

"Every Saturday night when he got drunk. Sometimes in between, if I didn't jump fast enough to suit him."

Derrick didn't like the kidnapper, but still, he kind of felt sorry for him. He couldn't even imagine his dad beating up on him or David. "Do you have a brother?"

"Nope. My mother ran off right after I was born, and nobody else was stupid enough to marry my father."

The kidnapper kicked one of the empty beer cans he'd just drained and sent it flying over Derrick's head. It landed in the part of the room where the table and chairs and kitchen stuff were.

"How come you don't put your cans in the trash like other people?"

"How come you don't mind your own business?" He pulled his cell phone from his pocket and started punching buttons. A few seconds and a bunch of cussing later, he hurled the phone against the wall. It broke into what looked like at least a hundred pieces.

"What did you do that for? You said you were going to call Daddy."

"Friggin' phone's used up."

"They don't get used up. Mom uses hers all the time, and it still works."

"Miss Becky has enough money to buy a better phone than I do."

"Just take us home, why don't you?" Derrick said. "My parents will pay the ransom, and then you'll have money to buy all the phones you want."

"I'll get the ransom. Don't you worry about that."

But the guy looked plenty worried. And mad. "So what are you gonna do now?" Derrick asked.

"Get another phone. I'll be out for a while. Don't try anything stupid. I won't be near as forgiving next time."

He shoved his burly arms into his ripped denim jacket and stamped outside, the key clicking as he locked the door behind him. Derrick waited until he heard the car drive away before maneuvering himself into a sitting position and turning toward the locked bedroom door.

"David, are you okay in there?"

"I guess so. I heard a car start. Did the kidnapper leave?"

"Yeah."

"Good. I hope he never comes back."

"He'll be back. He just went to get a phone so he can call Daddy. Can you get the tape off your wrists?"

"Nope. I can barely wiggle my fingers."

"Same here."

"If we had something sharp to rub up against, we could cut the tape off," David said. "You know, like a knife."

"Right," Derrick agreed. "Or any kind of jagged edge." He wiggled off the sofa and leaned against it for support until he got his balance. Once done, he started shuffling his way to the kitchen. "I'll check out the kitchen. You look around in there. But try not to fall. It might be hard to get back up."

"Okay, but there's not much in here."

Derrick should have better luck in the kitchen, but he'd have to work fast. One of the drawers was slightly ajar. He could see a knife inside it but didn't see any way he could pick it up.

A daddy longlegs scurried across the floor and crawled over his toes. He couldn't move his foot to kick it off. Another thing, the kidnapper had taken their shoes away from them so that if they escaped again, they'd have to run barefoot through the woods. Like that would stop them.

He needed a jagged edge, and he needed it fast.

SAM COTRELLA had been with the FBI for ten years now. He'd never planned to become a resident expert in dealing with child abductions. It had just happened over time, starting with his first kidnapping case in Ohio over five years ago.

Most of his cases had turned out well. A few hadn't. Those were the ones that came back to haunt him at moments like this. They were also the reason he knew there was no time to waste even though it was almost midnight.

He settled in the family den with Nick and Becky Ridgely and tried to size up the situation as best he could as they filled him in on the details. Becky's brother Zach, a local deputy, and her sister-in-law Shelly, formerly a CIA agent, were in the room, as well.

The rest of the family had left the room at his suggestion. Nick and Becky could fill them in later, but too many people talking while he was getting specifics often confused the issue.

"The man Langston talked to said you'd worked abductions before," Nick said once he'd given the rundown on what had happened and how they'd handled the situation to this point.

"Several. You might remember the Graham case in Houston last year."

"I remember it," Becky said. "A fourth-grade girl was abducted by one of her father's employees."

Nick looked puzzled. "I don't remember that."

"You wouldn't," Becky quipped. "It was during football season."

The tension in the room swelled to new proportions. Sam knew from the basic information he'd been given before arriving that the missing twins' parents were separated. He'd worked in situations like that before, too. The strain between them would not make this any easier.

"Julie Graham was the daughter of a Houston CEO," Sam explained. "A disgruntled employee with a history of mental illness abducted her from the park near their house while the nanny was tending to a younger sibling."

Nick leaned in closer, his muscles taut. "How did you get her back?"

"The father turned over the money at the agreed-upon time and location, and once Julie was safe, we came down on him with a SWAT team we'd put in place. The abductor tried to shoot his way out and was killed in the exchange of gunfire."

"I don't want gunfire," Becky said. "I don't want to take any chances."

"We never *want* gunfire," Sam said. "But the girl was never in danger. We'll negotiate a plan of exchange that focuses on keeping the boys safe."

"There's not much to negotiate," Nick said. "I have the money. He can have it. All I want is my sons."

"So what exactly do you expect from the FBI?" Sam asked.

"I want you to find David and Derrick in case the kidnapper doesn't call."

"My gut feeling is that he will call," Sam said. "He wants the money. That's what this is about. Otherwise he wouldn't have made that phone call about the ransom so soon after the boys were in his possession."

"That seems reasonable," Becky agreed. "But Nick told him we have the money and he didn't seem in any hurry to get it. And he wouldn't let us talk to the boys."

That worried Sam, as well. There could be several explanations for not letting them communicate with their sons but most obvious was that the boys were in no condition to assure their parents they were safe. No use to point that out. Both Nick and Becky were well aware of the danger their sons were in.

His goal now was to convince them that they needed his guidance all the way.

"If you do exactly as the kidnapper wants, we may not be able to protect your sons. That's why we need to negotiate and why you need to let me veto any arrangements for the exchange that I don't think are feasible."

Becky pulled her bare feet into the chair with her and hugged her knees close to her chest. She looked a lot like a vulnerable little girl herself in that position. Sam could only imagine how hard this had been on her—and the worst might be yet to come.

"The kidnapper promised that we'd get David and Derrick back safely if we cooperated," Becky said. "I guess we were fools to believe him."

"You were frightened parents," Shelly countered. "That's why we need Agent Cotrella's expertise."

"I'm still not sure how this works," Nick said. "Are you saying we should tell him you're from the FBI and that he'll have to negotiate with you? I'll tell you up front that if that's the plan, I don't like it."

Sam swiveled the desk chair so that he was looking directly at Nick. "The abductor won't even know I'm here. I'll listen in on the calls and guide you through the conversation by feeding you information, but you'll do the talking."

"If we put the phone on speaker, he'll immediately suspect police or FBI involvement."

Sam nodded. In spite of his reluctance to call in the FBI, Nick had a good grasp of the situation. "I have a two-man tech team on the way," Sam said. "They'll put attachments on the phone that will allow me to listen in to your calls without the kidnapper suspecting anything."

"Can they trace a cell call from a prepaid phone?"

"Maybe not to the exact location, but they'll be able to identify the general area where the calls are originating."

"And this equipment will prevent the kidnapper from having any inkling that his calls are being monitored?" Nick asked.

"He won't be able to detect any difference in the sound of his voice or yours."

"He's been calling Nick's cell phone," Becky said.

"We'll monitor both your cell phones and the house phone," Sam said. "He may change up in an attempt to keep you off guard. Now let's get down to the specifics of negotiation. Up to this point, you've let him make most of the decisions. It's time you threw in a few demands of your own."

Apprehension darkened Becky's blue eyes. "What kind of demands?"

"Make it clear to him that the plane will absolutely not leave the ground until the boys are back with you."

Nick bristled. "You're damn right it won't. The guy can't be so crazy he doesn't know that."

"Assume nothing. He may try to ensure his safe arrival in Mexico by taking one of the boys on the plane as his hostage."

"Surely, he wouldn't," Becky said.

"You'd think, but I had a case in Nebraska a couple of years ago where the kidnapper had abducted a sister and brother. He gave the parents the sister in exchange for the money and told him that once he was sure there were no tricks, he'd tell them where their son was."

"And did he?" Shelly asked.

"No. Once he had the money, he had no reason to

cooperate. He left the boy with an accomplice, who decided to ask for more money. That's when the FBI was called in on the case."

"Do we still provide the plane and the pilots?" Nick asked. "As per his instructions?"

"You can provide the plane. The FBI will take care of the pilots."

"Fine by me," Nick said. "But the boys will be released to me. I'll have it no other way."

Sam nodded. Cool-in-the-clutch Ridgely. That's how one sportswriter had described him. Sam had an idea that calm resolve would be tested as never before by the time this was over. But Sam's job went better with optimism. He would ensure the focus stayed on bringing David and Derrick home alive.

For Christmas.

For a brief second Sam let his mind wander to his own kids at home snuggled in their beds with visions of Christmas morning dancing in their heads.

He'd do all he could to make certain this had a happy ending, but the longer this took, the more the possibility of failure increased. The twins had already been in the hands of the abductor for more than thirty hours.

NICK PACED the small downstairs study that Sam Cotrella had chosen for his operations room. The guy seemed to know his stuff and didn't come off as too cocksure of himself. Nick liked that about him, the same way he liked those qualities in his teammates.

Teammates. That was another problem—minor when compared to his sons but nagging, nonetheless. They kept calling and trying to find out what in the hell was going on with him. They were baffled. A few were downright angry and had accused him of going soft and sabotaging their chances of making the play-offs.

The NFL was a business and multimillion-dollar receivers did not just up and walk out of a hospital without a doctor's clearance.

He'd stalled everyone off with feeble excuses. He was resting at home while the swelling went down and he got the pain under control. He'd miss Sunday's game but would be ready to work out with the team on Monday. Things were under control.

That was the biggest lie of all. It was 3:00 a.m. and still no word from the son of a bitch who had his sons. Things had never been more out of control. As for the rest of his life, that hell would just have to wait.

The house was quiet, but Nick doubted there was much sound sleeping going on. Every time he stepped into the kitchen for a cup of coffee, there was a new group of family members sitting around the table.

Growing up the way he had, he'd never even imagined there were families like the Collingsworths. They had their differences, but when trouble appeared, they stuck together like superglue.

He'd miss them when the divorce was over. Not the way he'd miss Becky. Not the way he already missed her, even with her lying a few feet away, sleeping restlessly on the brown tweed sofa.

His gaze fixed on her, and a potent ache clogged his throat, making it difficult to swallow. He walked over and covered her with the knitted throw that was lying near her feet. She snuggled into it the way she'd once snuggled against him on cold, wintry nights.

Before he'd let things deteriorate to the point she could barely stand to be near him.

A sharp pain started in his shoulder and crept into his back, growing worse when he tried to take a deep breath. He grimaced and started to the kitchen for a glass of water.

The piercing ring of his cell phone stopped him. His body grew numb, his feet frozen to the floor as he waited for the agreed-on signal from Sam to take a call. It was late. Not even his teammates would call at this hour.

The caller ID said Marilyn Close. He looked to Sam, who'd walked up behind him. "I don't know anyone by that name."

"Take the call anyway. The kidnapper could be using a stolen phone."

Becky jumped to a sitting position and grabbed for the earphones that would let her listen in on the conversation if the call was from the abductor. Sam's were already in place. He took a deep breath and took the call.

And then the panic he'd worked to keep in check exploded inside him. The voice was the kidnapper's, but Nick was certain something was seriously wrong.

Chapter Eight

"You're lucky those brats of yours are still breathing."

The abductor's voice slurred as if he were drunk or on drugs, his anger seeming to vibrate through the phone into Nick's brain.

"If you've hurt them, I'll kill you." The words left his mouth before he remembered Sam's orders that he was to wait for a nod or instructions before responding. Even if he had remembered, he doubted he could have held back.

"Your threats don't scare me, Nick Ridgely. Are you ready to pay up?"

Sam nodded.

"I have the money you asked for."

"All five million?"

"Yes, in fifties and twenties, just as you instructed. Now I want to talk to my sons."

"But you're not in control here, are you, big shot? So listen up and do exactly as I say."

Sam mouthed the words for him to insist.

"I'm not doing anything unless you let me talk to my boys," Nick said, keeping his voice dead level.

The abductor spewed a string of vile curses. "Then I'm through talking to you. Put Becky on the phone."

Nick's muscles clenched. His fury went nuclear and would have resulted in some curses of his own had Sam Cotrella not been there motioning Nick to give the phone to Becky.

Reluctantly he did so, exchanging the phone for her headphones as Sam made quick notes on the yellow pad he was holding in front of her.

She read his question into the phone with a control that surprised Nick. "Do I know you?"

"You did once. Back in your rah-rah days. Maybe we'll just have us a grand little reunion on that plane to Mexico."

Sam quickly scribbled the response. Becky read it into the receiver. "I don't know what you're talking about."

"I don't trust your husband. I want you on that plane with me when I flee the country—my insurance that I actually get to Mexico a free man with money in hand."

Nick mouthed the words "no way," but Sam was already scribbling a different answer on his pad.

Becky nodded. "Deal," she said. "But the plane won't take off until I know both boys are safe."

"That's the deal I offered."

"We can meet at the airport in Houston where my brother Langston keeps his private jet."

"No. I'll tell you where we meet. You have the plane ready to go. I'll call you and let you know when."

Sam scribbled. Becky read. "Why wait? What's wrong with now?"

"I got this high going on, baby. If you were here, we could be having a real good time. Guess that fun will just have to wait until we're on your brother's jet."

Nick grabbed a pen, wrote out his own instructions and pushed them in front of Sam.

Becky is not getting on that plane with him.

Sam waved him off and nodded to Becky to follow the instructions he'd just written.

"What time will you call?"

"When I'm good and ready. Have the money, a pilot and you. If there's anyone else present or if I even suspect you've called the cops in on this, the deal is off and the boys are corpses. You got that?"

"The boys can't just be left at the airport on their own. Nick will need to be there," she said.

"Fine, bring Nick. Maybe I'll get his autograph."

The man laughed as if this were all some big joke. If Nick could have gotten his hands on his throat right then, he could have strangled him without a second thought.

"Let me talk to my sons," Becky insisted again.

"They're not exactly with me right now, sweetheart. They're kind of tied up somewhere else, but don't you worry. They're just fine. But you should have taught those little brats some manners. If I wasn't so nice, they'd be in big trouble."

"Don't hurt them," she begged, this time speaking on her own. "We'll give you everything you ask. Just please don't hurt them."

But the kidnapper didn't hear her plea. He'd already broken the connection.

"We'll have to move fast on this," Sam said, already punching in numbers on his cell phone.

Nick wasn't giving in that easily. "I don't know what you're thinking, but Becky is not going anywhere with that scumbag."

"Of course not," Sam said. "All the people in that plane will be FBI. A dozen more agents will be on the ground either hidden from view or posing as airport crew. Now, can you get Zach in here? Shelly, too. I can use their help in taking care of a few things. While you're at it, get Langston as well so we can verify information about his aircraft."

"I want to be there when he releases David and Derrick," Becky said.

"We'll talk about it," Sam said as he started giving orders to whomever it was he'd called.

"I don't want you there," Nick said. He knew the statement had come out too much like an order the second he saw the rebellious expression on Becky's face.

"I didn't ask for your permission," she said.

"I know," he said, this time going for appeasement. "I just don't want to add to the risk."

Thankfully, she let the confrontation dissolve without an argument. The wheels were turning again. His sons, *their* sons could be home in a matter of hours. Nick wouldn't breathe easy until they were.

Then the rest of his life could come crashing down on top of him—one heartbreak at a time.

BULL DROPPED the phone to the seat beside him as he crossed the bridge heading back to the dilapidated cabin where he'd left the boys. He'd planned on buying another prepaid model from a convenience store in Livingston, but luck and fast thinking had saved him the money.

He'd stopped at an all-night truck stop on Highway 59 where he knew he could buy a fifth of cheap whiskey and some joints from the night manager. Under the table so to speak, though everyone in these parts seemed to know where to go for after-hours booze or a quick fix.

The phone had been easy pickings from a broad who'd stopped for coffee and left her phone sitting next to her cup and cigarettes while she went to the bathroom. He'd palmed it on his way out. She'd probably have it disconnected before he used it again, but that was okay. He'd stop at a pay phone next time—one on his way to meet Nick Ridgely.

The fifth of cheap whiskey was almost gone now. He shouldn't have started it before he made the call, but his head had been still pounding from the blow he'd taken from the boys that morning, and he needed something to kill it. Once he'd started, he'd stayed with it.

Women, drugs and booze. That had always been his downfall. But in a few more hours he'd have plenty of money to buy all he wanted. Not cheap booze or tawdry women, either. He'd have the best that five million could buy.

The car's wheels hit the shoulder and skidded completely off the roadbed. He yanked it back to the middle of the narrow strip of asphalt.

Slow down, buddy. Stay focused. Your next turn is coming up, and then it's just a few more miles back to the cabin.

The car swerved again. He could barely keep his eyes open, but he had to keep driving. He didn't dare leave those Ridgely brats alone any longer than he had to. They were his ticket out of here.

Just him, the pilot and Becky. He couldn't wait to get his hands on her—and all over her. She probably wasn't as hot as she'd been in high school in that sexy little cheerleading outfit. Firm little tits pushing at the fabric. He couldn't count all the nights he'd gotten his rocks off thinking of those.

She'd ignored him then. She wouldn't have that option now.

His turn was just ahead. He put on his brakes and slowed almost to a stop before turning on yet another winding, narrow road, this one dirt and half washed-out and with potholes big enough to bury a man.

Then a few more miles and he'd make the last turn onto the red clay trail that meandered back to the old fishing cabin. The place had belonged to his grand-pappy back before the creek had dried up and become clogged with logs and trash.

His dad had brought him fishing out here a few times when he was a kid. The last time had been his seventh birthday, but he remembered it as if it was yesterday. His father had gotten the poles and bait from the car, then proceeded to get falling-down drunk.

His dad had hooked him with the jagged end of his fishing hook, then kicked him until he was black and blue for crying when he yanked it loose, tearing a bloody hole in his flesh as he did.

It was the first time he'd thought about killing his dad, years before he actually did it. That had been a long, long time ago, and no one had ever suspected him of murder.

Bull's eyes closed. A second later he slammed into a tree.

"THE LAST phone call was made from somewhere in the area of Livingston, Texas, from a phone belonging to

Marilyn Close of Longview. I've got someone checking her out as we speak," Sam announced, once the entire family had gathered in the cozy kitchen. The room smelled of coffee and the spicy apricot coffee cake Lenora had just pulled from the oven.

"I bake and pray," she'd said. "My way of holding together."

He would never have called a family conference at 1:30 a.m., but apparently none of the Collingsworths had done much sleeping since the boys' abduction. Now that he had all four of Becky's brothers, plus a few of the women, in attendance, he was glad to have them aboard.

They not only worked as a seamless team but they were smart and all willing to do whatever it took to get David and Derrick home safely. Families like that didn't come along every day, especially when they were also one of the wealthiest families in Texas.

"It's likely the phone was stolen," he continued, "but at least we know the general area where the abductor must be holding the boys."

"I say we start combing that area for them at daybreak," Zach said.

"Can you take care of that while still keeping the kidnapping quiet?" Sam asked.

"Absolutely."

"Then go to it." Sam made a couple more notes on his pad.

Nick stirred a bit of cream into his coffee. "What about the fact that the man seems to know Becky? Shouldn't we be checking into that?"

"He didn't say how he knew me," Becky said. "He could have been lying."

"We can't assume he's lying," Nick insisted, "and if he does know you I don't see how he'll be fooled by an FBI agent who's impersonating you."

"You'd be surprised how easy that is to achieve," Sam said, "as long as we keep the agent at a distance until the boys are with you."

"Do we know who that agent will be?" Langston asked.

Sam nodded and sipped his coffee. "All taken care of. Her name's Evie Parker, and not only is she petite like Becky but she's a master with undercover disguises. She has her own collection of wigs in every color. When I talked to her, she said she could fool Becky's mother as long as she didn't have to stand too close. However, that might be a slight exaggeration."

"But she hasn't even seen me," Becky protested.

"She has your picture."

"How?"

"I snapped it with my cell phone and sent it to her. She's on her way here now, flying in from Dallas with our pilot. They'll land at the same place Langston keeps his private jet in case there's no time for us to get together before that. She'll get a car and drive out here from there if there's time."

Sam had a feeling there would be plenty of time and that this was not going to play out exactly as it was being scripted. Just a hunch, but his hunches had a history of being right more often than they were wrong. Agent's intuition.

That and the fact that the kidnapper had been drunk when he called. The guy was obviously losing control of the situation. The question was *why?* He hoped the answer had nothing to do with the physical condition of David and Derrick.

"He must have known Becky in high school," Jaime said, "assuming rah-rah days refers to her being a cheer-leader. She wasn't one in college."

"Good thinking."

"What can we do to help?" Matt asked.

"I need copies of Becky's high school yearbooks. I'd like her to peruse them and see if any of the guys stir bad feelings."

"My yearbooks are packed away in the attic."

Matt stood up. "I'll bring them down."

"I'll go with Matt," Bart said. "There are lots of boxes in the attic. Finding the right one could take a while."

Becky stuck a fork into the slice of coffee cake her mother had set in front of her. "I'm not sure what you mean by bad feelings."

"Perhaps someone you had problems with. Maybe a guy who had a crush on you that you didn't share. Maybe someone who aggravated you or even seemed creepy to you. We're grasping at whatever we can find," Sam admitted.

"I don't remember anyone like that attending Colts Run Cross High."

"Sometimes pictures can jog a memory. Have you ever been stalked?"

Becky hesitated. "Not exactly."

Not the answer Sam was expecting. "I'll need more than that."

She laid the fork back down and reached for the mug of hot coffee, sipping slowly before answering. "Right after I started college I met this guy in my freshman psy-

chology class who I could have sworn was following me
around campus. He never asked me out—not that I
would have gone. He had zero personality. But he always
seemed to be around, staring at me from a distance. It
freaked me out big-time."

"Did you say anything to him about your concerns?"

"I thought about it, but before it came to that, he
dropped out of school. But the really weird thing is, a
few weeks ago I saw a man who reminded me of him
in Colts Run Cross."

Sam saw the clench of Nick's jaw. Unless Sam was
misreading the signals, he was more tuned in to his
wife than Sam would have expected under the circumstances. And he was definitely protective of her.

His guess was that Nick Ridgely was not the one
who'd initiated the divorce, though he might have made
some dumb mistake that caused Becky to give up on
him. Men with hero status had temptation thrown at
them left and right.

Sam waited for Becky to elaborate on the man who'd
reminded her of the college stalker. She didn't. "Do
you think it could have been the same man?"

"I don't think so. It was more the feeling I got when
I noticed him staring at me than his appearance. Not the
old cliché about undressing me with his eyes, but more
like the one about spiders crawling across the skin."

"Did you only see him that once?"

"Yes, and then only for a few seconds. I'd stopped
at Thompson's Grocery to pick up a few items, and he
was checking out in front of me. I'm almost positive
he's not from around here. I would have seen him
before—or since."

"Definitely weird," Sam agreed. "I'll need a description of him and as many specifics about the psych class as you remember. I'll have someone check the school records and see if we can get a roster for that class. You may recognize his name if you see it printed."

"I can sit with her while she skims her yearbooks," Shelly offered. "I can jot down her description of the man she saw in the store and make notes on anyone else of interest."

"I'd appreciate that." It would relieve Sam to go over the exchange plans with the other agents who'd be involved. "And Nick, you and Becky should try to get a little rest as soon as she finishes taking a look at those yearbooks. I doubt we'll be hearing from the abductor again before morning. He's probably sleeping it off right now."

"Is that everything?" Becky asked.

"For now." But Sam would have felt a lot better about this if the kidnapper had let Nick or Becky talk to their sons. Not hearing their voices raised a whole new set of questions with possibilities none of them wanted to consider.

NICK WALKED to the family den and stared out the window as the dawning light of a new day dissolved the night.

Wednesday morning. Two days before Christmas. His heart twisted as if it were trying to wrench itself from his chest. Becky stirred from her position on the sofa but didn't open her eyes.

He'd tried to talk her into going to her room for at least a few hours, but she wouldn't venture that far from him and his phone. Not only did she want the chance to hear her sons' voices but she wanted to be there if the kidnapper asked to speak to her again. Had it been left up to her, she'd have willingly climbed on the plane with the kidnapper in exchange for David and Derrick's safety.

Except for Zach, he hadn't seen the rest of the family in the past few hours. Zach had to be running on empty, but he'd left a half hour ago to get started on trying to locate the kidnapper and the boys. Sam had the FBI on the mission, as well. To Nick, it sounded like trying to find a particular face in a game-day crowd of seventy thousand.

Still, Nick envied their chance to do something useful. He would rather be doing anything other than pacing and waiting for the damned phone to ring.

He walked to the bookcase and studied the rows of family photographs. He picked up one and held it closer so that he could make out the details in the dim morning light.

In it, the boys were no more than four. David was crawling through a pile of wrapped presents. Derrick was on tiptoe reaching to hang an ornament on the Collingsworth Christmas tree. One of the many Christmases Nick had missed due to being on the road for an upcoming game.

Not that they hadn't always celebrated again when he got home, but nonetheless, he'd missed the actual day the same way he'd missed lots of big moments in their lives. School plays. Derrick's first touchdown on the parks department youth team. David's first win in the local rodeo's youth barrel riding competition.

Becky had captured the moments for him on film. At

the time that had seemed enough. No. Who was he kidding? At the time, he'd been so involved with his own life, with the drive to win and the excitement of the upcoming game that what happened back home barely scratched his consciousness.

"What time is it?"

Becky's sleep-husky voice cut through his thoughts. When he turned, he saw that she'd kicked off the blanket and was sitting up, raking her fingers through her disheveled hair with one hand and clenching a throw pillow with the other. Her torment was tangible, a heaviness that filled the air like thick, poisonous smoke.

Nick glanced at his watch. "Six-twenty."

"You'd think he'd call."

"He's probably still sleeping it off."

"If he'd only let us talk to the boys, if I just knew they were safe, that they aren't being mistreated or abused, I could handle this."

"Don't think those things," he pleaded, though the same fears were eating away at him. He ached to drop to the sofa beside her and cradle her in his arms. In spite of his words about not contesting the divorce, it wasn't what he wanted. He wanted things to be the way they were in the beginning—when she loved him as much as he loved her.

Mostly he wished he had a chance to make up for everything he'd missed with his sons. He dropped to the edge of the leather hassock, waiting until Becky let her gaze lock with his.

Finally the question torturing his heart found its way to his tongue. "Am I a terrible father, Becky?"

BECKY FOUGHT the urge to lash out at Nick, to hurl all her frustration and fear at him. But it would only be a temporary release, a cruel, punishing sting that would do neither of them any good.

She opted to choose her words carefully. "David and Derrick love you," she said honestly. "You're their hero."

"A hero, but I'm not much of a caretaker. I'm not there for them to do the little things other fathers do, like go to their ball games or help with their homework, at least not on a full-time basis."

Surely he didn't expect her to contradict that. Yet one look into his haunted eyes, and she couldn't add to his guilt and pain. What purpose could it possibly serve?

"You love them," she said, willing to let it drop at that.

"It's not enough, is it? Not for the boys and definitely not for you. I'm away too much. You said it yourself a thousand times."

She dropped the pillow and clasped her hands in her lap. "It was never just your physical absence, Nick. Even when we were together during the season, you weren't really there. You pulled away emotionally. I know it sounds crazy, but I felt betrayed, as if football were your lover."

Nick shrugged and looked away. "NFL football is demanding."

"So is life, Nick."

And she had never been able to simply turn off their marriage and life together the way he had. Never once had she become so immersed in anything that she didn't need to reach out and touch him, if not in person then by letting their souls touch in some meaningful way on the phone.

Not so with Nick. It was as if they existed on different planets during football season, and the expanse of space that separated them couldn't be bridged. Not even when they'd made love. That had probably hurt most of all.

"Things are going to change, Becky. When we get the boys back, things will change. That's a promise." He reached over and took her hands in his.

"I hope so, Nick, for your sake and the boys." But he'd made those promises before, always when his back was up against the wall. To give him credit, he'd probably even tried to change. But then football season would start, and he'd fall into the consuming drive to be the best receiver in the league all over again.

"I just want the boys home safely," she said. "I can't think beyond that."

"I know." Nick reached up and tangled his fingers in her hair, his thumb brushing her earlobe.

It would be so nice to wrap herself in his arms and have him hold her. Just hold her, but she couldn't let herself. Her mother would say she was stubborn. Too much like Jeremiah.

But it was more than stubbornness that made her keep Nick at arm's length when she ached for the comfort of his arms. It was survival.

She looked up as heavy footfalls trod down the hallway and stopped at the doorway. Sam was standing there.

"There's been a new development."

The slump of his shoulders told her the news would not be good.

Chapter Nine

"We haven't been able to acquire the log from your freshman psychology class in college," Sam said, "but we ran a routine computer check on males who were in your high school at the same time you were there."

Becky sucked in a ragged breath. "Then I hope you found a more promising suspect than I did by looking at old yearbooks."

"We had some luck." Sam handed her a computer printout with two names followed by sketchy information obviously gleaned from police files. She scanned the data quickly.

The first one was Tim Gillespie, a male Caucasian who recently went bankrupt due to gambling debts he'd incurred along the Mississippi coast. The name was only vaguely familiar. She checked his age. "He would have been two years ahead of me. I don't actually remember him."

"Not surprising," Sam said. "According to what we have on him, he only lived in the area a few months."

"His family may have been migrant farm workers," Becky said. "We always had several of those who rotated in and out according to what crops were being harvested at the time."

"He's a long-shot suspect," Sam admitted. He tapped the second name. "What about Adam Leniestier? He's been arrested three times, always for some kind of get-rich-quick scam."

Adam she remembered well. "I dated him a few times my junior year," she said. "He was a con man even then, always a charmer and constantly trying to get someone to do his homework for him, but he was never in any real trouble."

"He's obviously progressed, but still guilty of nothing that's put him behind bars for any extended period of time."

Nick leaned closer to read over her shoulder. "Stealing credit cards from girlfriends and writing hot checks. That sounds worthy of a jail term to me."

"Not if he sweet-talks the girlfriends into withdrawing the complaint," Sam said.

Becky kept reading. "According to this, he did serve a few months for bilking FEMA out of money after Katrina."

"Right," Sam said. "He claimed he lost everything. Truth was he was living in New Jersey at the time."

"His dad still lives in Colts Run Cross," Becky said. "Mr. Leniestier goes to our church and works for the highway department, but Adam's mother divorced him right after high school and I haven't seen Adam since."

"Still, he sounds like the kind of man who might try to pull off a kidnapping." Nick slid the printout closer. "Except that it says here he's living in Denver now."

Becky considered the logistics. "If Adam got the

idea for the kidnapping after seeing you get injured on Sunday, he'd have had to move fast."

Sam nodded and rubbed the tendons in his neck. "We checked. There's no record of his taking a flight to Texas."

"He could have driven all night," Nick said, "or bought a ticket using a fake ID."

"Distinct possibilities," Sam agreed. "We're following up on him, but I don't think he's our man."

Becky got the impression Sam hadn't told them everything yet. "Is there another suspect?"

His eyes narrowed. "Do you recall a student in your class named Jake Hawkins?"

This time the name triggered disturbing memories. "I remember him."

"What can you tell us about him?"

"He moved to Colts Run Cross my senior year—too late to be included in the yearbooks. He seemed nice enough, but…"

"But what?" Nick asked when she hesitated, his voice hoarse and edgy.

"He never talked about his parents, but he moved in with his grandmother, Nancy Hawkins. She was a retired schoolteacher, the kind of teacher students loved to hate. Anyway, she died from a fall on her stairs right after Jake started living with her, and some of the kids claimed he murdered her."

"He was never arrested for that," Sam said.

"No. The police said it was an accident, but you know how rumors are. They just get started and take on a life of their own, especially since Jake wouldn't talk to anyone about the accident after that—not even at the funeral. I don't know where he went to live after his grandmother died."

Nick stepped away from Becky, but closer to Sam. "What do you have on him?"

"He spent three years in a state penitentiary for attacking a pregnant woman in a case of road rage on I-20 near Dallas. Apparently she rear-ended him, and he yanked her out of the car and stabbed her repeatedly with his pocketknife. The woman didn't die or lose the baby, but she spent a month in the hospital. Jake was paroled two months ago."

"Was he in the Huntsville facility?"

Sam nodded.

"So he's likely still nearby." Nick rammed his right fist into the palm of his left hand. "Damn. That's just the kind of lunatic who might kidnap two young boys on an impulse."

"Wouldn't his parole officer know where to find him?" Becky asked.

"Unfortunately, he's already broken the conditions of his parole by moving from his original address without letting anyone know where he was relocating."

"So he could be anywhere," Becky said.

"Yes, and unfortunately, there's more."

Her legs grew wobbly, and she dropped back to the sofa. More. Always more. "What now?"

"The prison psychologist was the only one who didn't recommend parole. He felt Jake was still capable of violence when provoked. He believed Jake to be emotionally unstable, prone to irrational rage and generally angry with the world."

Becky fought the burgeoning dread, but she had to face facts. "In other words, he's a dangerous sociopath."

"Find Jake Hawkins," Nick said. "I don't care what it takes. Just find him, or I will if I have to hire a whole damn army of men to track him down."

"We don't know that he's our guy," Sam reiterated.

"Find him anyway."

Given to irrational rage when provoked. And nothing would likely provoke him faster than finding out that they'd called in the FBI. And the longer this went on, the more likely he was to discover that fact.

Becky felt the stirrings of vertigo. Why didn't that damn phone ring?

"DERRICK."

Derrick jerked awake instantly at the sound of his name. His eyes darted about the room as he came to terms with where he was and why he couldn't move his hands.

He remembered turning the faucet with his head and running water over his wrists to try to loosen the tape. It hadn't worked. Neither had rubbing his wrists back and forth across the edge of the TV. He didn't remember falling asleep on the sofa, but he must have.

"Wake up, Derrick, and talk to me."

"I am awake." He held his breath expecting to hear the kidnapper yell at them to shut up. There was nothing. Surely the guy was still gone to get a phone. Maybe he wasn't coming back.

"What's going on out there?" David asked.

"Nothing." Derrick wiggled his way to a standing position and wished he could go to the bathroom. He needed to real bad. "Are you doing okay in there?"

"Kind of. Where's the kidnapper?"

"I don't see or hear him. I don't think he came back last night."

"Then I'm doing great. I have the tape off my wrists and almost off my feet."

"You're kidding, right?"

"No, I fell asleep, but then I woke up and started looking for something sharp. There's a nail sticking out of my headboard. I rubbed against it until I finally cut through the duct tape. Oh, jeez!"

"What's wrong?"

"The last of the tape came off my ankle. Felt like the skin was going to come off with it, but it's okay now."

Derrick heard a clunk that he figured was David sliding off the bed. He started working his way toward the door that separated them. He was glad he wasn't an inchworm that had to move this slowly all the time. He heard David rattling the doorknob.

David groaned and muttered a word their mother would have a fit if she'd heard him say. "I can't get out of here."

"I'm sure the kidnapper took the key with him." Even if he hadn't, Derrick couldn't have reached the padlock near the top of the door frame, and he sure couldn't climb on a chair with his feet bound.

Derrick had never seen a padlock on a bedroom door before, and he figured the guy had put it there just to lock them in.

"I'll have to break the door down," David said, "like the guy did in that movie we watched with Grandpa the other night."

"He had something to ram it with," Derrick said.

And he hated to say it, but the actor was a lot bigger and stronger than David.

"There's an old Indian statue in here. It's made of iron, I think, like that dinner bell Bart hung on the back porch. I can hammer the door down with it, I bet."

Derrick backed out of the way as the statue crashed into the wood. The old wood cracked and splintered. Not enough that he could see David through the hole, but a few more hits and he might be able to.

The statue crashed into the wood again, and this time there was an opening big enough he could have pushed his fist through it. The kidnapper would be super mad when he saw that. They'd best be long gone.

"Hurry," he called.

This time when the metal crashed against the door, the statue broke right through and ended up on Derrick's side. David grabbed the splintered wood and tore it away until he could climb right through.

"Grab a knife and cut me loose," Derrick said. "We have to get out of here before that stupid kidnapper gets back and goes ape."

"Yeah. We gotta move fast. He may be out kidnapping more kids."

"We'll escape and come back and save them."

"That would be cool. Then we'd really get our pictures in the newspaper."

"We might even get to be on TV."

David grabbed a kitchen knife from one of the drawers under the counter. Derrick turned so his brother could reach his wrists.

"Boy, this sure works better than a nail."

Derrick wiggled his fingers as the tape came loose,

and David peeled it from his wrists. "I'll do my own ankles," he said, reaching for the handle of the knife.

"Good, 'cause I got to go to the bathroom."

In practically no time, Derrick's feet were free, as well.

He gave a whoop and kicked one of the beer cans that littered the floor the way he'd seen the kidnapper do. It crashed into the wall and clattered to the floor as Derrick rushed to the bathroom to take care of business.

David was at the refrigerator when Derrick made it back to the kitchen. "There's a couple bottles of water," he said as he grabbed one and twisted off the top. "I say we drink this one and save the other until later."

"Okay. You drink first. Is there anything else in there?"

"Beer."

"Mom would kill us if we drank that."

"There's ketchup and some bread. We can make a ketchup sandwich. I like those."

"For breakfast?"

"Better than oatmeal."

Derrick pulled an opened package of pretzels from the cabinet. That was all there was except for a couple of cans of tuna with easy-open tops, some crackers and a package of uncooked lima beans. He stuffed everything except the beans into the pockets of his jacket just in case they got lost again.

David was waiting at the door. "I wish we had our shoes."

"I just wish we had a key," Derrick said, suddenly realizing that they'd have to break down the front door as well to get out of the house. He grabbed the Indian statue from the floor and had it hefted above his head when he saw David pull the rope from his inside jacket pocket. He let the statue slip from his hands and crash to the floor.

"Do you want me to break the door?" David asked.

"Not yet. I'm thinking maybe we shouldn't escape."

"Are you loony? I'm escaping and right now." David dropped the rope and grabbed the statue, grunting as he hoisted it over his head.

"If we run, we might just get lost again and the kidnapper could find us like before."

"And if we don't escape, we'll be stuck here with ketchup sandwiches for Christmas."

"Not if we're waiting for the kidnapper when he comes back. He thinks we're all tied up, so he won't be expecting anything." The plan kind of took shape as he talked. He liked it better all the time. "You could lasso him and pull him down, and I could hit him over the head with the statue and knock him out again. Then we could get the phone he went after and call Mom and Dad to come get us."

David held on to the statue. "What if I miss when I try to lasso him?"

"Then I'll still hit him and knock him out. I'll be behind the door. You can be perched on top of a chair, ready to throw the rope as he walks in."

"I don't know," David said.

"Well, I do. We'll outsmart him. You know, like *Home Alone*. That way we won't have to run around in the woods barefoot trying to find the way back to the highway."

"How are we going to tell Mom and Dad how to come get us when we don't even know where we are?"

"Then we'll call 911. They can find you anywhere. We'll be home in plenty of time for Christmas Eve."

David swung the rope. "Okay, but we have to get ready for action. The kidnapper might walk in that door any second."

Derrick's heart was beating fast. But they could do it. He knew they could. And it would sure feel good to see Mom and Dad walk through that door together.

He just wished the together part would last forever. Divorce was like having a "parent-napper" steal your dad and keep him for most of every year.

THE TWO MEN stamped along side by side. They'd been hunting together for more than forty years, ever since they'd married sisters. Their wives loved holiday gatherings. Hermann and Bruce loved getting away from the hustle and bustle and occasionally even killing a buck.

They'd gotten a late start this morning. Too much whiskey last night. Sun was full up now, but there was still time to bag a big one if they were lucky.

"What the Sam Hill?"

Bruce shouldered his rifle and stared into the woods. "I don't see anything."

"Over there." Hermann pointed toward the half-washed-out dirt road they'd driven in on. The front of a black car was wrapped around a pine tree.

"Lucky bastard if he walked away from that."

Hermann trudged toward the wreck. "Don't look like it's been there too long. Not rusted out—well, except for that spot on the back fender, and that's an old dent."

Bruce was fifty pounds lighter than Hermann, mostly

because the sister he'd married was a lousy cook. He overtook Hermann, reaching the car first. Hermann was only a step behind.

The driver was slouched over the steering wheel, not moving. Blood smeared the side window and was clotted in a clump of hair on the side of his head.

Hermann moved so as to get a better look. "This must have happened in the last few hours. If the man's dead, I bet he's not even cold yet. Color's too good."

He eased the door open. The smell of cheap whiskey and marijuana hit him in the face.

"Guess that explains why he collided with the tree," Bruce said.

"Yep. Poor bastard didn't even get to finish his stash." Hermann pulled two joints from the man's shirt pocket and stuffed them into his own. "For later." He felt for a pulse. "Heart's ticking."

"He's just sleeping off a drug and booze stupor. Do you think we should call for an ambulance?"

"If we do, we'll get stuck out here for hours waiting for them to show up and then have to talk to some meddlesome country bumpkin sheriff," Hermann said. "And we'll have to deal with this codger if he wakes up. And he ain't gonna be in a good mood when he finds I lifted his doobies."

Bruce leaned in and put a hand on the man's back. The man groaned and jerked but didn't open his eyes. "We could call 911, just in case he's hurt worse than he looks."

"If you call, they'll have your name and number, so you're still gonna get involved whether you like it or not."

"Guess you're right. Gotta wonder what he was doing out here in the middle of nowhere, though."

"Probably getting away from a wife who's a dry-hole gusher just like we're married to."

"You're not telling me nothing I don't know. Mary Sue can talk the horns off a billy goat." Bruce slid his hand down the back of the seat and lifted the injured man's wallet from his pocket.

"What are you doing now?"

"I'm just checking to see if he has some ID on him." He opened the wallet and looked in the money sleeve. "Guy's broker than we are."

"Well, I'm not contributing to the cause," Hermann said, his eyes already peeled for game. "Are we going to hunt or not?"

"Wait, here's an ID. A driver's license, just issued two months ago to Jake Hawkins. Age thirty-two. Address in Huntsville, Texas."

"That's not more than forty-five minutes from here. He'll find his way home when he comes back to the real world."

"Hey, what's this buried in the back?" Bruce pulled out two hundred-dollar bills and unfolded them. "What do you know? The guy's not totally busted." He started to refold the bills, then stopped.

Hermann put his hand on his brother-in-law's shoulder. "Are you thinking what I'm thinking?"

"Damn straight, I am. He's just going to waste it on booze and drugs. In a way you could think of it like we're doing him a favor to take it."

"If you put it that way…" Hermann grinned, though he felt a bit uneasy. He'd never stolen money before— unless you counted cheating on your taxes.

"One for me and one for you." Bruce handed Hermann his hundred. "Now, this is what I call a success-ful hunting trip."

"And we haven't even spotted a whitetail."

They walked off, not bothering to shut the car door behind them. A jaybird jeered from a tree branch over their head. A rabbit scurried from one thick clump of underbrush, only to disappear into another one.

And an elegant buck with an impressive rack stepped into the clearing mere yards away. Hermann found him in the sight of his rifle and poised his finger on the trigger.

But the crack of gunfire did not come from his gun. He spun around in time to see Bruce fall to the ground in a pool of blood. And then the second bullet fired.

ODORS OF COFFEE, bacon, sausage, eggs, grits and biscuits wafted from the kitchen as Nick and Sam joined the Collingsworth family in the dining room. It held one table in the house large enough for all of them to fit around. The table was new, but was an almost-exact replica built by Matt and Bart to replace the one lost in the fire and ex-plosion that had barely missed taking all their lives.

The Collingsworths had been through a lot togeth-er. It didn't surprise Nick at all that they would hang together in this.

Nick took the chair to the left of Becky while Zach's wife, Kali, squeezed into the chair on Becky's left.

"I talked to Zach on the drive over here," Kali said. "He's in the Point Blank area, showing Jake Hawkins's picture around and hoping someone there may know where to find him. But he's not mentioning the kidnap-ping," she added quickly. "He's saying the guy jumped parole, which is the truth."

"Good," Nick said. Not that they knew for certain Jake was behind the kidnapping, but he was definitely the most likely suspect that had surfaced.

"Did Zach get any sleep last night?" Becky asked.

"Not much, but Zach can go longer without sleep than anyone I know. When I was in danger last winter, there were nights when he barely closed his eyes."

Matt forked a couple of sausage patties from the serving platter before passing it on. "Bart, Langston and I are cutting out of here in a few minutes. We're all taking our own trucks up to the Point Blank area."

"To do what?" Becky asked.

"Help Zach. There's a lot of back roads up there and not a lot of extra deputies. It was Sam's idea," Langston said. "And it definitely beats sitting around here doing nothing."

Jaime pushed away from the table. "Why just you guys? I can drive and ask questions. David and Derrick are my nephews, too."

"You'll never pass for a deputy tracking down a parole jumper," Nick said.

"Maybe not, but I'll come a lot closer to getting men to talk to me than you guys will. And I can look like a deputy if I want. I have a pair of khaki chinos and a boring jacket I can wear." She turned to Sam. "What do you say Mr. FBI agent? Would you buy that I'm a deputy?"

"Not unless you're wearing heat on your hip."

"I not only have a pistol but I'm an excellent marksman," she said.

"And so am I," Shelly said. "I'll go with you."

"Is that a good idea?" Lenora asked.

"Time is of the essence," Sam said.

He let it go at that, but as far as Nick was concerned the solemnity in his tone said a lot more. The boys had been missing almost two full days now, and they hadn't actually talked to them since shortly after the kidnapping. They had the ransom. It was the kidnapper who kept changing his tune.

Something was obviously wrong. And if he knew that, so did Becky and the rest of her family. They were walking that thin line between anxiety and outright panic.

Nick managed to get down a few bites of food. Becky didn't. She stared into space as if she couldn't even bear to look at the spoonful of scrambled egg she'd put on her plate.

Nick hated to see her hurting like this, hated that he hadn't protected their sons better. Hated that the only comfort he could offer were empty phrases.

His phone rang. The room grew deathly silent. Nick checked the caller ID. "Out of area."

Sam nodded, and Nick took the call even as he, Becky and Sam hurried back to the study.

He answered with his name. "Nick Ridgely."

"Good. You're just the man I want to talk to."

His coach. Not the man he wanted to talk to. Nick motioned for Sam and Becky to ignore the call. "I'm sorry I haven't gotten back to you, but I'm involved in a family emergency that I can't leave. It should be resolved soon, and I'll rush back to Dallas the minute it is and have the MRI and the CAT scan the neurologist ordered."

"This isn't like you, Nick. Why don't you level with me about what's going on?"

"Would it help if I said this was literally a matter of life and death?"

"It helps. I really need for you to say more."

"Look, I know I'm breaking the terms of my contract. You can fine me whatever you think is fair."

"I don't want to fine you. I want you to check back in the hospital. From what I hear from the doctor, you're not only in danger of never playing again but of risking paralysis."

"I think he's overreacting, but I'll have the tests run. Soon. Hopefully tomorrow."

Nick glanced at Becky. Damn. She was still wearing the earphones. He didn't want to get into this with her. Not now. "I can't talk now, Coach. I'll get back to you soon."

"Don't wait too long."

"No. I won't." Nick broke the connection before Becky heard more. She'd already heard too much.

She stared at him with a haunted look in her red and swollen eyes that ripped away the last of his tenuous control.

"Were you ever going to tell me the truth, Nick, or was all that talk about you changing just another broken promise?"

She was right. If he was ever going to change, the time was now. Only, there were some secrets he could never share.

Chapter Ten

Paralyzed. It was a fear every wife of a professional football player lived with, but it had never seemed this frighteningly real. Becky clasped the back of a chair. The nervous adrenaline she'd lived with since the boys' disappearance dissolved, throwing her balance off kilter.

"You told me you were fine," she accused, "that all you needed was a few days' rest."

"You had enough to deal with without adding my troubles to the list."

"Your troubles? You make it sound as if we're talking about the common cold." She struggled for a deep breath to steady her emotions and clear her mind. "You should be in the hospital."

"No, I should be here. The tests can wait until the boys are safe."

"I don't get it," she said, trying to make sense of the incredible. "You were in the hospital from early Sunday evening until Monday noon. Surely that was enough time for them to do a CAT scan and an MRI."

"The machine was down, so that had to wait until

morning. And then the team decided to fly in a neurologist from California who specializes in sports injuries resulting in severe trauma to the neck and spinal cord. He wanted to be there to supervise everything."

"So they did nothing for you that night?"

"They gave me pain medication, kept me comfortable, took X-rays. The usual."

"But no prognosis of any kind?"

"The E.R. doctor said I most likely had a central spinal cord contusion. That's not necessarily serious."

No, not serious at all. Only possible paralysis. "Don't gloss over this as if I'm worrying over nothing. I may be your wife in name only at this point, but I'm still your wife. I think I deserve to know exactly what the doctors told you in the hospital."

"In the first place, I'm not glossing over anything. I've set my priorities. Getting the boys back is number one on that list. In the second place, I've had MRIs and CAT scans before. The doctors order them if there's any doubt. It's called preventing malpractice suits. Their worries never amounted to anything before, and I don't expect them to this time. I know my body. I'm not in that much pain."

He nailed her with a penetrating stare. "And in the third place, you're my wife in name only because you chose for it to be that way. You stopped living with me. Stopped letting me touch or make love to you. You're the one who filed for divorce. I've fought it every damn step of the way." His voice had become strained, hoarse with emotion.

He was right on all counts, but he was the one who'd repeatedly shut her out of his life, just as he'd done again by keeping his medical condition from her—as if it were none of her concern.

Her heart twisted, and a raging need settled in her chest. She didn't know how she felt anymore except that she couldn't bear to think of Nick's being seriously injured. "I don't want to argue with you, Nick. Just tell me what the doctors told you."

"Fair enough." He crossed the room and stepped into her space, so close she could feel his warm breath as he took her hand and pulled her into the chair she'd been using for support. "Sit down, and I'll explain what I know."

He pulled a chair up close to hers. "I took a bad hit. I'm not denying that."

"I know. I saw the replay." And the horror of watching him motionless for long, agonizing minutes was a feeling she'd never forget. "You must have been in terrible pain."

"I didn't feel anything. That's what made it so alarming for me and the trainers who rushed onto the field."

Even admitting that much was a first for Nick. He always had to be tougher than anyone else, thought any sign of weakness on the field was for rookies or sissies.

"When did the feeling return?"

"Not until I was at the hospital and through with the X-rays. I told you that on the phone when you called."

"Exactly what is a central spinal cord contusion?"

"If you want the medically correct description, you'll have to go to the doctor for that."

"I'll take layman's terms. I just want to know what you're up against."

"I'm up against a possibly deranged kidnapper."

"Nick…"

"Right. You want facts. Your way. As best I can understand it, a spinal cord contusion happens when something thumps the spine and a bruise occurs. If it improves, no problem."

"And if it worsens?"

"Then the circulation to the spinal cord is affected."

"And you could wind up paralyzed." She shuddered and clasped her hands tightly to keep them from shaking. She'd thought she could handle this, but the images of Nick as a paraplegic or worse were making her physically ill.

Nick took her balled-up hands in his. "It didn't worsen, Becky. I'm here with you. You can see that I'm fine."

"Then why is the doctor who called yesterday and your coach so concerned?"

"The doctor is concerned that the spine might still be unstable and that if it were to receive another blow, it could still slip and cause complications. But, he doesn't know my body like I do. I've taken thousands of hits. I'd know if this were more than a routine injury. I'll go in and have all the tests he wants when the boys are safe. For now, just trust me with this."

Hot, salty tears burned at the back of her eyes. Their marriage might be over, but Nick was the father of her sons. She'd never stopped loving him. That's not what the divorce was about.

Nick caught an escaping tear with a brush of his thumb on her cheek. "How did we get here, Becky? How did we get to the place where we can't touch or hold each other when faced with the most frightening time in our life? And I'm not talking about my injury."

How? She'd gone over and over those reasons both with him and in her own mind, but at this minute, they didn't seem all that important. They would matter again when all of this was over. When David and Derrick were safe. When Nick was back on the playing field going on with his life, that didn't include her.

But right now, she needed him so much it hurt. She slipped her arms around his neck and held on tight.

BULL HAD the mother of all hangovers. It felt as if someone were hammering nails into his skull as he dragged the men's bodies into the woods. He hadn't intended to shoot them. He'd just gone nuts when he realized they were robbing him.

Blown a fuse the way he had on the highway that day when the pregnant woman had cut in too close and forced him into the guardrail. That's how it was with him. Something snapped and he went crazy. Drinking and drugs made it worse.

He'd made a big mistake getting drunk and high last night when the biggest deal of his life was in the making. Five million dollars ransom for a couple of bratty boys he wouldn't have given two cents for. He should have already made the exchange by now. Should be in Mexico drinking a margarita with a pretty *señorita*.

Instead he was sweating like a pig and trying to cover up a couple of stupid murders. The man was heavier than he looked, and Jake's arms ached from maneuvering the deadweight through the heavy underbrush. And after this he still had another one to go. Then he'd have to find a way to cover up the blood. It wouldn't do to have the bodies found before he was long gone.

He had one of the men's phones and a set of car keys. He wasn't sure where their vehicle was parked, but he doubted it was far from here. Their boots weren't muddy enough for them to have been out here long. Besides, with that little shower they must have gotten while he was out of it last night, their trail should be easy enough to follow.

Too bad it hadn't rained before those Collingsworth kids had escaped. He could have found the little snots in no time and saved himself a lot of trouble. But he didn't have to worry about them now. They were tied up and locked in. They weren't going anywhere without him.

All he needed was to make the call to Nick Ridgely and have them meet him at Lone Star Executive Airport in Conroe. But he'd have to move quickly. In fact, he should make that call right now and then just bury the phone with the bodies.

Once these corpses were found, this area would be crawling with cops. He damn sure wasn't going back to prison on double murder charges. A man could die behind bars for that.

Which meant if there were any complications before the exchange, he'd have to kill the Ridgely boys so that they couldn't identify him. And then he'd find his own way to Mexico. He'd be poor, but poor and on the run beat death row by a country mile.

EVIE PARKER arrived just after 9:00 a.m. carrying a medium-size tan piece of luggage and a grim expression that fit the chilly undercurrent that hung over the big house like a dark shroud. She was petite with ash-blond hair, razor cut to hug the nape of her neck.

Becky was immediately impressed with her professionalism and her warmth. Those two traits didn't always go hand in hand. She wasn't sure about her ability to take Becky's place in the plane, however. Their size was similar. Their facial features weren't.

"What's with the paparazzi outside your gate?" Evie asked once the introductions were over. "Did word of the kidnappings leak out?"

"They're here hounding Nick," Sam explained. "He's a star receiver for the Cowboys. He was injured in last Sunday's game."

"My brother-in-law Matt Collingsworth assigned a few Rangers to guard duty to keep the media hounds at bay," Nick said. "The cowboys didn't hassle you when you arrived, did they? I'd told them we were expecting you."

"They were very efficient. They checked my credentials and waved me right through."

Trish brought a plate of warmed coffee cake and a pot of coffee to the study as Sam caught Evie up to speed on the negotiation progress or lack thereof and on the attempts to identify and locate suspects.

Evie sipped the coffee. "Then you don't have a real lead as to Jake Hawkins's whereabouts?"

"Not yet," Sam acknowledged. Crumbs showered his shirt as he bit into a chunk of coffee cake. He brushed them to the floor with the palm of his hand. "But he's only a suspect at this point. We have nothing to tie him directly to the crime. All we know is that he has a criminal record and he went to the same high school as Becky."

"For a few months," Becky added.

"So our best bet would be to get a call from the kidnapper," Evie said.

"I couldn't agree more," Becky said. "But one other thing while we're on the subject. No matter who the kidnapper is, if it turns out he has seen me recently, I find it difficult to think he'll believe you're me."

Sam leaned back in his chair. "That's only because you haven't seen Evie's disguise mastery at work. Once she's done, even Nick may have difficulty telling the two of you apart."

Becky motioned toward the suitcase. "And everything you need for that transformation is in there."

"No. Some will come from your closet and dressing room. I'll wear the outfit you choose and apply your makeup. My bag contains a couple of blond wigs that I matched to your picture and materials for altering my facial features."

"You can alter your facial features?"

"Nothing dramatic, but minor adjustments. I took lessons from a Hollywood makeup artist who's worked on a lot of major films. You'd be surprised how easy it is to acquire a specific look. But I don't think we'll have to do much altering this time. Makeup, hair and clothing will pretty much do it."

Becky still had her doubts. "I guess seeing is believing."

Nick pushed up the sleeve of his black T-shirt and glanced at his watch. "How long will this transformation take?"

"I like to have an hour, but I can work faster if I have to."

"I once saw her put on twenty pounds and some serious wrinkles in under twenty minutes," Sam said.

"Was the kidnapper fooled?"

"Yes, and she managed to take his gun away from him and apprehend him. He's still in jail."

Becky's cell phone rang, startling her and running clawing fingers over her nerves. She checked the ID. "It's a friend from Colts Run Cross," she said, letting it ring. She'd avoided taking most of her calls since the boys' disappearance. Eventually she'd have to return some of them but not yet. Making small talk under the circumstances would be torturous if not impossible.

Evie finished her coffee and set her empty cup on the desk next to Sam's. "Shall we get started, Becky?"

"I'm ready, but still a bit apprehensive about your taking my place on the plane."

Sam rubbed his chin thoughtfully, though his facial expression never changed. "Evie has to take your place, Becky. It's too risky for you to go with the kidnapper. I couldn't guarantee your safety."

"I'm not worried about *my* safety."

"I am," Nick said.

Not his call, but she wouldn't argue the point until she saw what Evie could do with a wig and some war paint. "I'll have the walkie-talkie with me." She held it up to make her point. "Let me know immediately if the kidnapper calls."

"Absolutely," Sam said. "Hang in there. We're making progress, whether it seems like it or not."

She wasn't fooled. He might keep up an optimistic front, but the ticking clock was wearing down all their confidence, his included.

Nick followed her to the door. When they reached it, he took her hand, tentatively as if expecting her to yank it away. "I know you're uneasy with this, Becky, but you can't get on that plane with that crackpot. Don't even toy with that idea."

She tried to pull away, not wanting to argue with him and knowing she could make no promises.

His grip tightened. "Be reasonable. The boys will need you here with them." He met her gaze, his own fears written in every line of his face. "So do I, and I can't face going through all this again while you're riding the wild blue yonder with a lunatic."

He was talking like a husband, as if the bonds between them were strong and loving. She wanted to trust that, but his need for her had always been short-lived, dissolving completely when football season claimed his mind, body and soul. Only now his season might have come to a permanent end and…

And she couldn't deal with any of this now. The stakes for her sons were too high. She took the stairs with Evie, praying with every step that her boys were safe.

NICK'S CELL phone rang at exactly 10:18 a.m. The caller ID said Hermann Grazier. He didn't recognize the name, but something deep inside him shouted that this was the call he'd been waiting for. This time he didn't wait for Sam's thumbs-up to answer.

"Nick Ridgely," he said, answering with his name as he frequently did.

"It's time for the show."

Adrenaline rushed Nick's system, speeding his heart until it felt as if it might burst from his chest. He pushed the button on the walkie-talkie to let Becky know the kidnapper had made contact.

"I'm ready," Nick said.

"Then listen and get this straight. One screwup on your part and you'll be burying your sons for Christmas."

Nick had never hated a man more. "Which airport?"

"Lone Star Executive in Conroe."

That would work. In fact, Langston had already mentioned it as a possibility. Langston would fly them by a helicopter—which was already waiting on the ranch helipad—to the small reliever airport northwest of Houston, where his plane and the FBI pilot by the name of Pete Halifax and two additional agents were waiting. Then it would be a very short hop to Conroe.

"We can meet you there in an hour."

"You do that. Have the money and the pilot on the plane with the engine running. When I show up, have Becky standing near the plane. I'll release the boys when I see her, but I'll be armed. One foul-up and I'll shoot to kill. I'll get at least one of the three before you get me. I might even get lucky and get them all.

"I'll call when I get there, and you can direct me to the waiting jet. Just remember. Double cross me once I'm on that plane and bang bang, your sons' mother is dead."

Sam nodded at Nick for him to accept the conditions.

"Everything will be just as we agreed," Nick said. "Now, let me talk to my sons."

"I'd like to do that, Nick, I really would, but we have a little problem."

Nick's fists knotted. His stomach followed suit. "What kind of problem?"

"They're not exactly with me at the moment. They're much too annoying for me to hang out with all the time. You really should teach them some manners."

"Where are they?"

"Telling you that would kind of void my bargaining powers, don't you think?"

"I want to talk to them and know they're safe and that you actually still have them before I turn over the money."

"You'll know soon enough. Meet me at the airport, Nick. My rules. No cops. One hour."

Nick was reaching for Sam's rapidly scribbled note when the connection went dead.

"I'm calling him back," Sam said. "Demand he let you talk to David and Derrick."

One touch of the sophisticated machinery Sam was manning had the kidnapper's phone ringing. There was no answer.

Becky yanked off her earphones and dropped them to the desk. "We're doing what he said. I don't care what either of you think. They're my sons. He says they're safe, and I have to believe that."

Sam grimaced. "Not the best scenario but this is manageable. So, you heard the woman. Time for the games to begin. The boys should be home by dinner."

Nick could sense Becky's apprehension, though she'd become more animated than at any time since this had all begun. He hated that he wouldn't be with her for the ride to Conroe, but she'd be with Sam. He'd keep her safe.

They went over the plans again. Sam would call the shots outside the plane. Pete would be the one in control inside the plane. Pete would pretend to have a problem while preparing for takeoff. As soon as the kidnapper was distracted, the two agents hiding in the food compartment of the plane would rush out, and between the four of them, they'd disarm and apprehend their target.

It sounded simple, but Nick knew that just like a Sunday game plan, one mistake could turn victory to defeat. But unlike a football game, failure to succeed could be deadly.

"I'll get Langston," Becky said.

"Right," Nick agreed, "and tell your mother to rev up the Christmas plans. This is going to be the best Christmas in the history of all Collingsworth Christmases. And I don't plan to miss a second of it."

Nick put out a hand to Sam as Becky disappeared through the door. "If we get David and Derrick back safely, we'll owe it all to you. Now, just take care of my wife. I'm leaving her in your hands."

"I'll do my best. She's a terrific woman. You're a lucky man."

"Damn lucky."

But luck or not, he might end up losing her to a ridiculous divorce. He didn't know how to keep her. And he couldn't call in the FBI for that.

Chapter Eleven

Becky felt miles removed from the action and frustrated with her inability to know what was going on. She was standing at a window in a cargo company facility that was owned by the family of one of Bart's fraternity brothers during his college days.

Nick had explained that with the paparazzi clamoring after him since his accident, she was merely trying to avoid unwanted attention and endless questions while waiting to board a chartered jet. Perhaps that was why the workers had pretty much ignored her except for offering a soft drink when she'd arrived.

She sipped the diet cola from the can and shifted for a better look at Langston's plane. She was too far away to see any movement around it except for two businessmen climbing into a jet belonging to a local charter service.

She checked her watch again. Ten minutes past the appointed time. Still no sign of the kidnapper or David and Derrick.

Nick was on the plane with Evie and Pete. She'd learned from Sam on the way here that Pete was a top-notch agent who'd been a fighter pilot in the navy before leaving the service to join the Bureau. Sam claimed that he, Evie and the two agents who were hidden away were the perfect team to apprehend the abductor.

Sam was inside the waiting area, just a few yards away from the plane, posing as a businessman waiting to catch a charter flight.

Her phone rang. She recognized the number as Sam's and murmured a breathless hello.

"I just heard from Pete. There's been no word as yet. Nick wanted me to let you know."

Frustration rolled in her stomach and ground along her nerve endings. "He should be here. We did everything he said."

Only, that wasn't quite true. He'd ordered them not to call in law enforcement. They'd gone to the FBI. "Maybe he knows he's being set up."

"That's extremely unlikely. Don't start panicking, Becky. We have what he wants. There's no reason not to be optimistic."

None except that her sons were nowhere in sight. Her cell phone beeped. "I'm getting another call."

"It's probably Nick, though he'll be calling on Evie's or Pete's phone. We're leaving Nick's open for the kidnapper."

"Okay. Keep your fingers crossed. Keep everything you have crossed." She broke that connection and took the incoming call.

"All systems are go, here. Are you okay?" Nick's voice was strained, though he was obviously striving for upbeat.

"No," she answered honestly. She checked her watch

again. Time had never moved so slowly. "Maybe this isn't the right airport."

"It's the right airport. Lone Star Executive in Conroe, Texas. He was perfectly clear on that. Take deep breaths and try to stay calm."

"Not going to happen."

"You've been great so far, Becky. Don't fall apart when we're this close to having the worst behind us."

If the demented abductor showed up. There truly was no reason for him not to, yet the dread seemed to be swelling inside her like an angry virus that was consuming her lungs. "Let me know the second you hear something."

"Will do. And, Becky…" His voice became a raspy whisper that faded to silence.

"What is it?"

"When this is over, when the boys are safe, we need to talk about us."

Her heart seemed to burst to life only to immediately shrivel back inside the cocoon where she'd hidden it away over the last painful months. They were both vulnerable now. Afraid for their sons. Treading panic. Double jeopardy for him with his future in football so unsure.

But she couldn't bear to start thinking their marriage could work again only to have those hopes slashed the second he went back to the team. Filing for the divorce had been like cutting her heart from her body. She'd put up a front during the day only to cry herself to sleep on countless nights, aching to crawl into his arms one more time. But she needed more than he could give.

She took a deep breath wishing it could steady her soul. "We'll see." She couldn't promise more than that.

"HERMANN GRAZIER is a construction worker who lives in Livingston, Texas. His wife is a schoolteacher at a public elementary school. They have two children, a boy aged twelve and a girl aged nine. No criminal record and no reason to think he is involved in the boys' abduction."

"Any explanation for how the kidnapper came in possession of Mr. Grazier's phone?" Nick paced the small plane as he carried on the conversation with Zach, his eyes constantly peering out the window for any sign of David and Derrick. Their arrival was officially—he glanced at his watch—forty-six minutes past due.

"Mrs. Grazier says he had the cell phone last night when they went out to dinner. She knows because he called his mother from the restaurant. She thinks he took it with him this morning, but when she tried to call him, there was no answer."

"Where is he supposed to be today?"

"Deer hunting with her sister's husband. Her sister's family drove over from Birmingham, Alabama, yesterday for the Christmas holidays. They take turns visiting each other's homes every year and the men always spend at least one day hunting."

"Tradition." Nick mumbled the word, then wondered why. He couldn't care less about Hermann Grazier's traditions, and he was sick to his soul of clues that went nowhere and negotiations that were ignored.

Damn. He'd preached staying calm to Becky, but he was losing it fast. "Where is he hunting?"

"His wife didn't know, but the phone call came from somewhere near Oakhurst, Texas, just a few miles east of the area where the last call was made from. There have been no calls made on the phone since the one made to you by the kidnapper. And if the phone is turned on at the present time, it's lost the connection with the network."

"So basically we know nothing."

"I'm working every angle I can, while I'm saddled with keeping the kidnapping a secret."

"It won't matter anyway if this exchange takes place." Nick almost choked on the *if*. This had to take place. Everything the kidnapper had asked for was ready and waiting. Accompanied by FBI agents, but he was certain the kidnapper didn't know that. If he had, he'd have never set up the meeting to start with.

"You still think we should have gone with the AMBER Alert and full-scale search, don't you, Zach?"

"What do I know? The boys will probably come hopping across the tarmac toward the plane any minute now. We'll all be celebrating back at the big house by dark."

It sounded good. But the clock was ticking. The drive from the Oakhurst area where the call originated to the airport in Conroe shouldn't have taken more than an hour tops. "Did you give the information you just gave me to Sam?"

"I did. He's the one who gave me Pete's number so I could call you. I knew you'd be keeping your line open."

"Have you talked to Becky?"

"I did, but I didn't mention anything about Hermann Grazier to her. She's a meltdown waiting to happen. I'm not sure how much more she can take."

Neither was Nick and that was slicing away at his control like the sharp edge of a machete. They needed action. They needed their sons' boisterous antics. Needed to hear their laughter ringing in their ears.

They needed one lousy break.

He finished the conversation and went back to pacing. After another hour had passed, even Evie and Pete had given up on trying to reassure him.

Two hours later the kidnapper had still not made contact. Nick walked away from the plane and called Becky. He needed to hear her voice. Most of all he needed her with him. He didn't have to go back on the plane. He could drive her home, and Sam could ride with Pete and Evie.

He made the call, but he was too late. Jaime had already come for her and was driving her back to the big house. He'd call her on the way home, though. It was time they pulled out all the stops.

Nick picked up his pace as he walked to the area where Sam was waiting. From out of the blue, something felt as if it had snapped in his back and white-hot pain shot up his spine. The doctor's warning echoed in his mind. He ignored it. The negotiations were a bust, but he couldn't give up. He had to find David and Derrick. For them. For Becky. For anything in life to ever matter again.

"I'VE LOOKED in every pocket. He doesn't have a phone."

Derrick dropped the cold rag he was using to soak up the oozing blood from the kidnapper's shoulder. "He has to have a phone. That's what he went after."

"Well, he must have just bought whiskey instead."

The kidnapper mumbled something that sounded like

more of the bad words he'd been shouting before David had stuffed a cotton washcloth into his mouth to gag him.

Derrick picked up the almost empty roll of duct tape and tossed it to the sofa. The kidnapper was on the floor, right where he'd fallen when David had lassoed him and yanked him down like a mean calf.

Derrick had done the real damage, though, popping him over the back of the head with the Indian statue. Well, mostly he'd caught his shoulder, but it had left him howling in pain while Derrick bound his wrists and ankles just the way the kidnapper had bound theirs yesterday.

Then, just to make sure he stayed put, they'd tied the end of the rope to the leg of the sofa. He'd have to drag that around with him if he moved. Pretty cool. Derrick couldn't wait to tell his friends how they'd tricked the grown bully.

"I bet Janie Thomas tries to kiss me at the Christmas pageant when I tell how we captured this jerk," Derrick said.

"Ugh."

"I won't let her, but I bet she'll want to."

"How come she'll want to kiss you? I'm the one who lassoed the kidnapper."

"Yeah, but you wouldn't pick her for your kick ball team in PE."

"She can't catch. Can't kick, either."

"But she's hot."

"You don't even know what hot means."

"Do so."

David scratched the itch where the tape had irritated his right ankle. "Forget Janie. What do we do now that there's no phone?"

"We'll have to try to find our way back to the main road."

"What if we just get lost again?"

"We won't," Derrick said. At least he hoped they wouldn't. It had been pretty scary out there roaming around lost, especially in the dark. "But this time we won't have anyone chasing us. The kidnapper will be right here waiting on the cops."

The kidnapper started flopping his body around. His face got so red that Derrick thought he might be choking. He pulled the rag from the guy's mouth.

The man spit on the floor and then started cursing them out again.

David got down on one knee and held the rag over the man's head. "If you don't quit saying all those bad words, I'll put the stopper back in."

The man spit again, this time aiming it at David. It missed, and it ended up dribbling off his own cheek. Served him right.

"Neither one of you have a lick of sense. If you did, you'd be bargaining with me for part of the five million your parents are paying to get you back."

"Yeah, right, like our parents have that kind of money."

"You're Collingsworths. Your family has more money than God. Just your daddy's bonus is probably in the millions."

"That can't be right," David said. "Mom said those skateboards we wanted were too expensive."

"And that we were too young for them," Derrick added, to be fair.

"She's just stingy," the kidnapper said. "Anyway I already called them. They're on their way here right now to bring me the money and take you back to the ranch. I say you get this tape off of me and we make a deal."

"I say you're crazy," David said.

"Yeah, why would we even believe you that our parents are on their way here?"

"Did you think I was just going to keep you brats around forever? That's the whole point of a kidnapping. They give me ransom money. I give them you, and then I walk away."

That part made sense. And if Momma and Daddy were on their way here, they'd be the crazy ones if they went off and got lost again trying to find their way to the main highway or to find help.

Derrick motioned to David to follow him outside.

"You could buy a lot of skateboards with your share of the money," the kidnapper called after them. "And I'd sneak it to you so that your parents would never know you were involved. You'd be the richest kids in school."

"No way! Janie Thomas is the richest kid in school. Her dad owns the grocery store."

"Well, at least give me a drink of water before you leave."

"We aren't leaving—not yet anyway. And there's not any water except that gross stuff that comes out of the tap." And Derrick and David were way too smart to drink that stuff.

"There's plenty of bottled water. You just have to know where to find it. There's some food, too. Untie me, and I'll tell you where it is. You help me get the ransom. I help you. It's the way the world works. Smart kids like you should know that."

They ignored him, stepped onto the porch and closed the door behind them. A clap of thunder rattled the windows of the cabin. The wind had picked up, and the clouds turned dark. It was going to rain again. They'd get soaked if they left now.

"Do you think he's telling the truth about our parents coming to get us?" David asked.

Derrick knocked a cricket from the rickety banister. "I don't know. He didn't come back with a phone, so I guess that means he could have used a pay phone to tell them where to bring the money."

"He left here in that old black car and came back in a new one." David walked down the steps and leaned against the vehicle. "What do you make of that?"

"I don't know. Maybe he stole it to make his getaway after he gets the money."

"Football players do make a lot of money, so maybe Daddy is going to pay the ransom." David hurried back to the porch as the first drops of rain splattered his head.

"I guess we could wait a little while and see if Momma and Daddy come. It's not like the kidnapper is going to do anything to us now."

"Right," David agreed. "No way we'd be stupid enough to cut him free, and if he tries anything, I have his pistol."

"Which we should probably keep with us at all times." Instead of on the table where they'd left it when they came out here. Lightning lit up the gray sky followed by booming thunder. The rain fell harder.

"If we go now, we'll get drenched anyway," Derrick decided out loud. "I don't want to be sick during the holiday break."

"Me, either. Let's go see if we can find that water. Or I'll have to start drinking the rain."

"Food would be good, too."

"Yeah. I can't wait to get home."

BECKY TRUDGED the few steps, hating to step into the big house. Her family would try to console her, but they'd feel the same crushing sense of fear and defeat that had haunted her since she'd first realized that the kidnapper was not going to show.

Lenora opened the door. She pulled Becky into her arms and, though she was no doubt trying to be brave, her hot tears wet Becky's neck.

"Please, Mom. I know you mean to help, but I can't handle this now. I just need to be alone."

"I understand, sweetheart. But you can't give up. We'll find the boys. We'll all help, and we won't give up until David and Derrick are back here with us."

Words. Just words. The smell of chocolate chip cookies hit Becky's nostrils and sent her stomach into feverish rolls. She ran for the bathroom, making it just in time to fill the toilet with green bile and the little nourishment she'd been able to force down that day. When she could hold her head up without the bathroom spinning, she went to the sink and splashed her face with cold water.

Reaching the towel, her fingers brushed a crystal bowl filled with shimmering red and gold ornaments. The sight of the bright decoration sent her over the edge, and before she could stop herself, she'd swept the bowl to the tile floor in a crash of broken glass and a stampede of rolling iridescent balls.

She sank to the floor, her body gripped by mind-numbing shudders. A crimson stream trickled down her leg. She'd cut herself, but she didn't feel anything but the scream gurgling in her throat.

The bathroom filled with people. Someone's arms went around her shoulders. Someone's hands tended her wound. The bile rose up in her throat again, and a wave of nausea gripped and tightened her stomach.

"Leave me alone. Please, just leave me alone."

"I'm here now. I'll take over."

Nick's voice rose above the noise and confusion.

"Go away," she said.

He didn't. The others did.

Tears were streaming down Becky's face now, and her heart felt as if it had died inside her chest.

Nick's arms wrapped around her, and he lifted her as if she were a small child.

"It's okay, baby. You have every right to cry, throw fits, scream. You do whatever helps."

She closed her eyes tightly and buried her face in his chest as he carried her up the stairs. The fight slowly went out of her but not the heartbreak of knowing every second that passed was taking her sons further away from her.

Nick pushed into her bedroom, yanked back the pale yellow coverlet and laid her on the sheets. "You need some rest. Lenora's calling the doctor to see if he'll pre-scribe something to help you sleep."

"I don't need pills. I need David and Derrick to come home."

Nick sat down on the bed beside her. "I just talked to Zach. He's following our latest dictates and going full speed ahead now like you told him you wanted when the kidnapper didn't show. The sheriff's department has put out an AMBER Alert and is faxing pictures of the boys to every law enforcement office in the state. He and Sam will coordinate the investigation together from this point on."

"This is some kind of bitter reprisal against one of us, Nick. It has to be someone who hates us and wants to get back at us the way Melvin Rogers did when he tried to blow up the big house with all of us in it."

"Melvin failed. So will this man."

"But this man has our sons." She started to shake again, the sobs beginning somewhere deep inside her and fighting their way to the surface.

Nick kicked out of his shoes and climbed into bed beside her. He wrapped around her spoon-style, his broad chest fitting against her back. Just like old times. Only nothing was like old times and would never be again. She grabbed quick, sobering breaths and then pulled away.

"Please just let me hold you, Becky. I can't do this alone. Neither can you."

She ached to slide back into his arms, but the cold bitterness of reality wouldn't let her. She turned to face him, clinging to the same stubborn pride that had kept her going even before the boys were abducted.

"I wasn't the one who tore us apart, Nick." She was being a shrew but this all hurt so much. She couldn't hold all her feelings inside and not choke on the anguish. The kidnapping. Knowing that Nick's need for her could never last. "You chose football over the boys and me. You chose being a star over being a husband and dad."

"It was never like that, Becky."

"Then how was it, Nick? Tell me how it was when you decided to treat me as if I were as invisible as the cheers you craved, because it felt like total rejection to me."

"IT FELT LIKE survival to me, Becky."

Nick slid his feet to the floor and walked away from the bed, stopping at the window and staring into the dismal, gray afternoon sky. She'd never be satisfied short of the truth, never be satisfied until she sent him back to the darkest corners of his miserable youth.

Not that he'd ever fully escaped it. Not that he could and therein lay the roots of all their problems. He'd tried desperately to move past his tainted history, had buried it so deep that not even the news media had discovered it.

But the shame was still inside him, taunting him and reminding him that he would never be good enough for Becky. That he'd never come close to measuring up to Collingsworth standards.

Her brothers could always be counted on to do what was right. They'd never turn their back on a woman in trouble. Simple truths they lived by. The basics that set them apart from the crowd.

Well, he wasn't a Collingsworth and never would be. He should just accept that and let Becky go on with the divorce and on with her life.

Becky sat up in bed, her eyes wide and accusing. "Just admit it, Nick. Say I wasn't enough woman for you. Say you deserved someone like Brianna Campbell to sport around and play celebrity with. Tell me there were dozens of Briannas. Damn it, just say something."

"Brianna? You think our problems have something to do with the likes of her?"

"She was in your hospital room when I called."

"I didn't invite her. She just showed up."

"But you have been dating her."

"A friend of hers is going out with one of our running backs. The four of us had dinner together one night. If that constitutes a date, then I'm guilty. But dinner is all it was." He shoved his hair back from his face and went back to stand at the head of the bed.

"I could have lots of women, Becky. It goes with the territory. I've never wanted anyone but you, not since the first night we…"

The first night they'd made love. The memories rushed his mind now, so intense his body reacted in unwanted ways. He concentrated on killing the telltale stirrings that would only make this worse. "There's never been anyone but you, Becky."

She shivered and wrapped her arms around her chest. "I almost wish there had been other women, Nick. They would have been easier to compete with than football."

He nodded, knowing she was right on some level even though it wasn't what she thought. "Football wasn't my mistress, Becky. It was my life, at least I thought that until faced with losing David and Derrick."

He wrapped his hands around the bedpost, wishing he had a football in them right now. Only he might never have one in them again, at least not as an NFL player. He was losing everything. How the hell could the truth hurt him anymore?

"I'm not who you think I am, Becky."

"What are you saying?"

"My father didn't die while fighting insurgents in the Middle East. My mother didn't die of cancer."

"I don't understand."

No, how could she? She knew only the fabricated version of his life, the fairy tale he'd concocted when he'd gone to live with the last foster family. His muscles bunched and throbbed as his thoughts hurdled into the past.

"My father attacked my mother in a drunken fit of rage when I was six years old. It wasn't the first time he'd hit her, and I'm sure it wouldn't have been the last. Only this time I was going to protect her. I went to the kitchen and got our longest knife.

"But I wasn't fast enough. When he slammed his fist into her stomach, she stumbled into the knife I was holding. I was going to protect her. Instead I killed her."

Becky slid from the bed and stood beside him. Her face had turned pale but her shoulders were squared, her stare unrelenting. "Why didn't you tell me this before?"

"The same reason I never told anyone. I wanted to forget it had ever happened. I thought about telling you time and time again, but you're a Collingsworth. Your family reeks of perfection. I didn't want your pity or theirs. I never wanted anyone's pity. Football made sure I never got it."

"But that was all so long ago, Nick. You've proved yourself over and over since then. Besides, you were just a kid, and none of that was your fault."

"You'd think, but it doesn't work that way. Football was the only thing I ever truly excelled at. It made me feel like I was somebody. And once I'm on the field I can't settle for less than perfection. No matter what I know logically, it's like I'm driven, the same as when I played high school and then college ball. I have to be better than everyone else to be good enough."

"You should have told me. It would have helped me understand."

"I'm telling you now. I want a chance to make us work, Becky. Just a chance, that's all I'm asking. But a real chance where you live with me even when things get tough, and you don't go running back to the ranch."

She leaned into him, resting her head on his chest. He circled her with his arms and buried his face in her sweet-smelling hair.

"Oh, Nick. I want to say yes, but…I need time," she whispered, finally pulling away.

It wasn't the answer he wanted. But it was probably better than he deserved.

Becky's phone rang. She grabbed for it and checked the caller ID. "It's Zach."

"HAVE YOU found out something new?" Becky asked before Zach had opportunity to return her greeting.

"I'm not sure. Some kids on four-wheelers out riding in the area near where the phone call was made found a car with its front end wrapped around a tree. They called the information in to the local sheriff's department. Two deputies are there now."

"That's all? Just a wrecked car?"

"I think the car may be the one used to abduct David and Derrick."

A collision would explain why the kidnapper didn't show. But… "Where are the boys? Have you checked the local hospitals? Was there blood?"

"We're checking the hospitals now. There's no sign

of blood in the car, but the vehicle fits the description of the one that picked up the boys on Monday, and deputies have found two pairs of kids' sneakers in the floor of the backseat."

"What size? What brand?"

She swallowed hard at Zach's answers. "The shoes have to be theirs, Zach. I'm coming out there."

"That's not necessary. You should stay home in case the kidnapper makes contact again. Besides, there are law enforcement personnel on the scene, and I'm heading there with Bart and Matt as we speak. I'll keep you abreast of any new information as soon as I get it."

"No. I'm coming out there." She might not be any help, but if her sons were in the area, then she wanted to be there, too. "I'll need exact directions."

"Okay, but let me talk to Nick first."

"I don't need his permission."

"I know that."

She handed the phone to Nick and went straight to her closet, stretching to her tiptoes to reach the plain overnight bag she'd bought this fall. She had no intention of coming home until this was settled and she had her sons.

She dropped the bag to the bed, then leaned over Nick's shoulder to see what he was writing on the notepad she kept on her nightstand.

"Directions to the wrecked car," he mouthed without taking the pen from the paper.

Hopefully that meant she'd get no argument from him. She left him on the phone with Zach and went to the bathroom to start packing the basic necessities. Her reflection in the mirror stopped her cold.

She looked ten years older than she had before the

abduction. New wrinkles had made deep grooves around her puffy eyes. Her cheeks looked sallow, her lips drawn, the bottom one cracked. She'd always chewed on it when she was nervous. And she was worlds beyond nervous now.

A light rain splattered on the bathroom window. She'd best take boots and rain gear. But the boys didn't even have shoes. The thought sent her determined attitude plummeting back to the abyss of dread.

But if they'd found the kidnapper's car then the boys had to be nearby.

Maybe wet. Maybe hungry. But safe. She wouldn't allow herself to think of them any other way.

When she returned to the bedroom, Nick was studying his notes. "We can be there in approximately an hour," he said, as if their going together was something they'd already agreed on.

"You can't go, Nick. You have to stay here with Sam."

He shoved a stray lock of her hair behind her ear. "Sam can come along if he likes, but I've had it with waiting around for this lunatic. I'm going after David and Derrick. I wish to hell I'd done that in the first place."

"You have to think of your neck and spine, Nick. You should stay here tonight and rest."

"My neck and spine are nonissues in this."

"Not according to Dr. Cambridge or your coach."

"Let it go, Becky. I'll check with Sam and let him know what's up. Can you be ready to leave in fifteen minutes?"

"I can be ready in ten."

"Have your mother and Jaime pack some sandwiches and a couple of thermoses of coffee, enough for your brothers and anyone else involved in the search. This might turn into a long, cold, wet night."

He started to walk away, then stopped to touch her cheek and let his eyes lock with hers. His gaze was penetrating and questioning. "I won't let you down, Becky. I hope you can believe that."

Her breath caught. He'd bared his soul to her, and now his eyes were pleading with her for something in return. A look that told him things had changed between them. A promise that she could start fresh.

She wanted so badly to give it. Already she felt her walls crumbling. But she'd built up those expectations time and time again over the last ten years only to have them sink into pools of regret. Would they ever be able to get past the heartbreak?

"I LIED to you," Bull said. "Your parents aren't coming out here to get you. Obviously they don't think you're worth the ransom. Now that I've seen what brats you are, I can see why."

"You better stop lying to us, or you're gonna be sorry."

Derrick knotted his little fists as if he thought one of them could actually cause Bull misery. His punch couldn't. His and his brother's stupid cowboy and Indian trick had. But they hadn't done as much to blow the deal as those two bodies in the woods were going to do.

Bull had been certain he could trick the boys into setting him free, but they were as smart and determined as they were devilish. They weren't going to buy into his schemes, and they weren't going to give him a chance to escape—not as long as David was pointing

Bull's own gun at his head. The little imp would be just spunky enough to shoot him, too.

He couldn't break free as long as they were in the cabin. That's why he needed to get rid of them. If a couple of eight-year-old boys could cut their way out of tightly wound duct tape, then surely he could do the same and a lot quicker.

Time wasn't on his side. If he hadn't given in to the rage and been so quick to pull that trigger, he could have still pulled this off.

But dead bodies brought cops, and the leaves he'd piled over them had surely washed away in the rain. That left him one option.

"So you kids gonna hang around here with me all night?"

"Nope," Derrick said. "We're leaving now, and when we come back, we're bringing our daddy and our uncles, and you will be sorry you ever kidnapped us."

He was sorry already, but they wouldn't be bringing anybody back. Once they were out of here, he'd free himself, then escape and track them down. He'd kill both of them before they had a chance to identify him. Luckily he had the hunters' rifles stuffed in the trunk of their Jeep. A pistol belonging to one of the men was still in the glove compartment.

He watched as they pulled on their jackets and got ready to leave. They were probably nice enough kids when they hadn't been kidnapped. Too bad they had to die so young.

Chapter Twelve

Jaime started filling the everyday glasses with ice water. "I don't know why we even pretend to have meals. It's not as if anyone is going to take more than a few bites. Even Blackie's not eating."

"We need food," Lenora said, "especially Jaclyn. Pregnant women can't do without proper nutrition." And Lenora needed the routine of familiar activities that required no concentration. She could have prepared the soup and ham sandwiches they were having tonight in her sleep—if she were doing any sleeping.

She'd finally dozed off a couple hours ago only to be wakened by a nightmare starring the boys.

"Are we eating in the kitchen again?"

Lenora nodded. The kitchen had a warmth the dining room lacked except when the whole family crowded around the big oak table.

"How many place settings do we need?"

"One for everyone who's not out searching for David and Derrick—except Jeremiah." Fortunately Lenora's father-in-law was still taking his meals upstairs, though he was feeing much better today.

Pulling him into this would add another layer of strain on all of them—especially Jeremiah. He'd made a miraculous recovery from his massive stroke over a year and a half ago, but she certainly didn't want to risk another one.

"I thought Kali went back to her ranch," Jaime said.

"She did, but only to check on her horses. She said she wouldn't be long. And Jaclyn is watching Randy while Trish is horseback riding with Gina."

"I'm glad," Jaime said. "Gina really needed to get out of the house for awhile. She had her own meltdown today when we got the news that the kidnapper didn't show."

"No one mentioned that to me."

"Because you have enough on your own plate, Mom." Jaime stopped to kiss Lenora's cheek as she sashayed by her with silverware.

So they were protecting her the way she was trying to protect them. Sometimes terrible things like this tore families apart. This one seemed to be pulling them all together. If it did that for Becky and Nick, it would be a blessing. But nothing would feel like a blessing until the boys were safe.

"I think we should all be out searching," Jaime said.

"I know you do. You've said that a dozen times over the last hour."

"We always pull together when something bad happens in this family. I don't see why it should be any different now."

"Zach thinks the situation is better left in the hands of law authority. Too many cooks spoil the broth."

"My nephews aren't broth. And all my brothers are out there helping. And so is Shelly."

"Shelly is ex-CIA. And she's in Zach's office in Colts Run Cross doing record checks at the moment. I'm sure you could go sit there and watch her."

"No, thanks. Watching the show is not my game."

And never had been. If Jaime was involved, she usually was the show. She had never been good at taking orders, and she had a way of claiming far too much attention from cops or any other men who happened to be around—even when she wasn't trying.

Lenora ladled hot tomato soup into a blue pottery bowl. "Zach has serious doubts that the kidnapper is still in the same place that he made the calls from. He thinks he may be regrouping to make another attempt at claiming the ransom."

"Well, if we don't hear something positive soon, I'm driving up there even if I'm just in the way. I can't stand sitting around here like a helpless female."

A spoon slipped from Jaime's hand and went clattering to the floor. She picked it up and tossed it into the sink. "I can't stand the thought of David and Derrick spending one more night with that crazed monster."

A loud thump behind her startled Lenora so badly she spilled soup from the ladle, bathing her fingers with the hot liquid.

"What the hell are David and Derrick doing with a crazed monster?"

Lenora turned just in time to see as well as hear Jeremiah's banging of his cane. "I didn't know you were coming down for dinner."

"Don't change the subject. What's this about David and Derrick?"

Jaime handed Lenora a towel to wipe the soup from

her fingers and took over with the ladling. "Might as well come clean with him, Mom. It is what it is."

And put bluntly, it was a living nightmare. Lenora collapsed into one of the kitchen chairs. "There's bad news," she said. "Sit down, and I'll tell you about it."

"I can listen standing up."

"Fine." It never did any good to argue with Jeremiah. "David and Derrick were kidnapped from school on Monday."

His wrinkles folded in on themselves, and his chin quivered. "Kidnapped?"

"Yes, while they were walking from the school to the church."

His face turned the color of chalk as he sank into the chair kitty-corner from hers. "Who took them? What does he want?"

She fed Jeremiah the details as succinctly and as calmly as she could, but there was no way to paint the picture that it didn't come out in shades of gray and black.

Jeremiah stopped her after practically every sentence with questions, but he was taking this much better than she'd expected. In fact, after the initial shock wore off, his face took on the defiant hardness he was famous for.

Once he'd exhausted her supply of information, he hammered his cane against the floor again. He hadn't been using the cane much of late, but apparently the flu had weakened him to the point he felt he needed it.

Odd, but tonight the sharp pounding Lenora used to dread seemed entirely appropriate. Welcome, even. A replacement for the scream of frustration she'd wanted to give all afternoon.

Jeremiah hammered again, the echo of it reverberating off the walls of the kitchen as the back door slammed indicating at least part of the family had returned.

"That kidnapper is messing with the wrong dad-burned family this time. He's swallowed himself a bitter pill there'll be no recovering from."

Lenora put a hand over his thin, heavily veined one. "I pray you're right."

"Of course I'm right. All the Collingsworth men are out there with their hackles up looking for him. Becky and Nick, too. The devil and Tom Walker couldn't stop them from getting David and Derrick back."

Jaime walked over and put her arms around Jeremiah's neck. "I like the way you think, Grandpa."

Trish joined them in the kitchen, balancing her young son on one hip. Gina, Jaclyn and Kali were a few steps behind her. They all stopped and stared at Jeremiah as if waiting for the proverbial second shoe to drop.

"Grandpa was just telling us how big a mistake the kidnapper made in going against the Collingsworths," Jaime announced.

"And I'm not talking just the adults," Jeremiah added. "I'd be willing to bet David and Derrick have given the man fits, too. Those boys have spunk. It's in their genes. No one should ever underestimate a Collingsworth."

Gina started the applause and the others joined in with the spontaneous approval of Jeremiah's much needed reassurance of faith in the family.

Lenora was thankful for it. As usual, Jeremiah was right. They would find the abductor, and he would pay.

And in a perfect world they would get the boys back safely.

In this world that just might take the miracle she'd been praying for all along.

IT TOOK AN HOUR to reach the area where the car they believed to be the kidnapper's had been wrecked. The car was registered to Jake Hawkins, purchased for twelve hundred dollars on time from a sleazy used-car lot the week after he got out of prison. It smelled of whiskey and marijuana and mold.

The CSI team was still on the scene, working in the misty rain and gusty wind, searching for evidence to link the car to David and Derrick. They'd shown Becky the shoes, and she'd verified they belonged to her sons or at least were perfect matches for the ones they'd been wearing when they'd left for school on Monday.

After that, both she and Nick were forced to watch the process from her car. They couldn't see much, but it was as close as the detective in charge would let them get. It was clear he didn't see any reason for their hanging around.

Becky was losing patience, and her stress-and-fatigue-laced headache was not making things any easier. As far as she was concerned, a lot of people were standing around doing very little instead of searching for her sons. She'd complained about that every time anyone got close enough to listen. They all assured her they were doing their jobs.

But ever since they'd arrived, she'd had a feeling, almost a premonition, that the boys were nearby. She knew how saying it aloud would sound, so she'd kept it to herself, but she felt it. Their presence seemed almost as tangible as Nick's, who was sitting next to her.

Finally Zach pulled up and parked next to them. He got out of his truck and slid into the backseat of her car. "Rotten weather."

"Damn the weather. Is anyone looking for David and Derrick?" she demanded.

Zach took off his wet hat and set it on the seat beside him. "Half of Texas now that we've alerted them."

"I don't see any sign of that."

"It's difficult to see past your nose in this weather, but a half-dozen deputies and your other three brothers are all combing the area and have been for the last few hours. They're checking every house, cabin and mobile home they can find.

"And the state highway patrol is setting up a roadblock on the highway to stop and search all vehicles leaving this area."

"The kidnapper's car is wrapped around a tree. What good does it do to check vehicles?" She wasn't even trying to fight her frustration now.

Zach leaned forward and massaged her shoulders. "Take it easy, sis. Getting riled at the cops isn't going to help. The kidnapper is either still holed up in the area or he's already cleared out. If he's here, we'll find him. If he's left the area, we have to depend on law enforcement agencies around the state to track him down."

Becky pressed her fingers into her temples, where the throbbing ache was building to an explosive crescendo. "It's not enough."

Nick reached over and put a hand on her thigh. "You need to get some rest before you bite someone's head off."

"He's right," Zach said. "You can only go so long without sleep. Why don't the two of you drive into Huntsville and get a room? That way you can be nearby and still get some rest."

"In other words, you're telling me to do nothing." She started to get out of the car but was hit with a wave of vertigo. She was sick, exhausted and now dizzy. Maybe getting some rest did make sense.

"What about you, Zach?" Nick asked. "What are you doing the rest of the night?"

"I'll be out here a few more hours, checking for any houses or cabins we've missed. We're working from a grid. The major areas have been covered, but there are a few seldom used back roads we haven't hit yet."

"I'd like to join you. I'll need to drive Becky into town first. I don't want her driving these dark roads alone when she's as tired as she is tonight, but I can meet you after that."

"Are you sure that's what you want to do?"

"Positive."

"Then why don't I get one of the CSI guys to drive Becky into Huntsville and make sure she gets checked into a room. They'll be through out here shortly."

"There's no need for that. I can go wizz you two," she said.

"Would you listen to yourself?" Zach exclaimed. "You're so tired you can't talk straight. You've been living on raw nerves and strong coffee for almost thirty hours. I'm not trying to get rid of you, but if you don't get some rest, you'll end up in the hospital."

"Okay, but I don't like leaving."

"I'll go arrange for a ride for you." Zach opened

the door and scooted out of the car without waiting for a response.

Nick took her hand in his and squeezed gently. "I'll go with you if you need me."

"You need your rest more than me, Nick. You're the one who's injured. You already should be in a hospital."

"When the boys are safe."

She knew it was useless to argue about this. "I'll be fine alone," she said. "You do what you need to do."

Zach returned a few moments later, the arrangements apparently made. "They're saving you a room at Whistler's Bed and Breakfast Inn. Steve Jordon will drop you off, and he says it's the most comfortable accommodations in this part of Texas."

Zach gave her a hug. So did Nick. And then he kissed her. A quick kiss, but it was the first time their lips had touched in months. She'd almost forgotten the taste of him. Sweet. Salty. Nick.

"I'll join you in the room in a few hours," he said. "Get some sleep."

"I'll try."

She closed her eyes and imagined the boys walking out of the woods and strolling toward the car. And then it was the four of them—Becky, Nick, David and Derrick running hand in hand through a soft summer rain.

ZACH GUNNED his engine, spitting gravel as he drove away from the mobile home where the inhabitants had told them about a recent break-in. The single wide was set in a clearing at the end of a ribbon of dirt and mud that looked more like a pig trail than a road, but this area was full of those.

Most led to deserted cabins, many built years ago before some river Zach had never heard of dried up. At least that was the word from the local sheriff, a giant of a Texan with arms like a gorilla's and thighs as big around as Zach's waist. His disposition was all snarl and growl, and Zach suspected that his bite was just as bad.

Nick reached for his seat belt as Zach's truck rocked and rolled through a couple of mud holes big enough to drown a large dog. "Do you think it's possible that the kidnapper was the one who broke into those folk's mobile home Monday evening?"

"It's possible, but it's hard to believe a man who'd put as much thought into how he wanted the ransom paid and how he'd planned his escape would risk alerting the cops of his whereabouts for ice cream and sodas."

"But then ice cream, sodas and spaghetti do sound like David and Derrick," Nick said.

"That's why I told him we'd like to check the house for fingerprints. I think we can get a team on that first thing in the morning."

"I'd like to think it was the boys and that somehow they'd escaped the kidnapper and were on the run. But if that were the case, why would he have called this morning and set up the meeting at the Conroe airport?"

Zach turned on the defroster. "Maybe he thought he could pull it off even without the boys?"

"And then changed his mind?"

"I'm just thinking aloud," Zach admitted. "The most likely scenario is that he was hiding out in one of these old cabins until he wrecked his car. He probably intended to steal a vehicle and close the deal this morning."

"But something stopped him."

"And if we knew what that something was, we'd have a handle on things and a hell of a lot better chance of finding all three of them."

The rain was more of a deluge now, and Zach was starting to seriously feel the crunch of a long day. Fortunately they had almost covered every inch of their grid—or rather unfortunately since they hadn't located the kidnapper.

Zach came across another road, this one in even worse shape than the one they were currently on. He was pretty sure it hadn't made the grid. He turned down it anyway, though he half expected it to ramble around a few curves and then dead-end into an overgrown patch of mud, grass and brush.

He hit a spot where the water from the rains completely covered the road, and he had to creep through it. Lightning cut a jagged path through the dark clouds followed by rumbling thunder. The weather might be about to get a lot worse.

Nick put his head next to the side window. "Did you see that?"

"The lightning?"

"No, but when it lit the landscape, I saw a house— or what's left of one off to the right."

"How far off the road?"

"I couldn't tell. I just got a glimpse."

Zach slowed to a stop and yanked the gear into Reverse. He backed up until he was in about the same spot they'd been in when the lightning struck. Grabbing his rain gear and a high-beam flashlight from the backseat, he opened the door. He was half out of the truck before he decided to grab a second gun from beneath his seat.

Nick did the same, and as soon as the ponchos were over their heads, they tramped through the slosh, their boots sucked into the muddy goop with every step.

Nick found the cabin again with the beam from his flashlight. Rundown. Leaning. But there was a vehicle parked in front of it.

Zach's adrenaline level spiked. "Looks like someone might be around."

"If they are, they're either already in bed or sitting in the dark. Unless the storm knocked out the electricity."

Zach's hand rode the butt of his pistol as they approached.

"A Jeep Cherokee," Nick said once they were close enough to get a good look at the vehicle. "Isn't that what Hermann Grazier's wife said he was driving?"

"Exactly."

"Maybe Hermann and his brother-in-law found this old cabin and took refuge from the storm."

"Except that they should have been out of here long before the worst of the storm started. And this vehicle's obviously been parked here since before the rain made a lake of the driveway."

"Makes sense."

"That's why I make the big bucks." The comment was more habit than joke. Nothing about this situation was a laughing matter. If the hunters were inside, Zach was pretty damn sure they hadn't ended up here willingly.

He doubted they were. But Jake Hawkins just might be. Which meant the boys might be inside, as well.

"Take this," he said, passing the extra gun to Nick. "I know you know how to use it. I've seen you on the driving range at Jack's Bluff. Keep your eyes peeled, and use the car for cover in case someone inside heard us approach."

Nick took the gun. "You think this could be it, don't you?"

"Yes, if by 'it' you mean that this could be where Jake Hawkins has been hanging out."

"I'd give anything to walk though that door and find David and Derrick alive and well."

"I know, but don't count on it. The place looks empty. And about the gun, I guess I don't have to tell you not to shoot unless it's a matter of life and death—then make sure you're not the dead one."

"Got it.

The hood of the Cherokee was up and rain was pouring into the car's guts. Zach failed to come up with a rational explanation for that.

"Work your way around to where you can see the back of the cabin just in case someone tries to escape that way. And stay protected."

Nick followed the order without question, staying low and near the tree line. Zach sprayed the front of the house with light, eventually letting the beam pinpoint the entrance. Gun poised for action, he walked up and knuckle-rapped the door.

"Police. Open the door and keep your hands in view."

Of course there was no response. That would have been way too easy.

He knocked and yelled the order again, sure that this time he'd shouted over the wind and rain. Still nothing.

Mentally and physically geared for an ambush, he tried the knob and the door swung open.

He flicked on the light, keeping his back to the wall and his trigger finger ready. There was no movement, but chaos painted a vivid picture that left no doubt in his mind that his nephews had been in this cabin with the kidnapper. They weren't here now—unless…

A shadow moved outside the open front door. He was not the only one around.

Chapter Thirteen

"Back up. Don't shoot."

"Damn it, Nick. I told you to watch the back of the cabin."

"Nothing going on back there." And Nick had far too much at stake to be hanging around outside. "I'll cover. Let's search the house."

With each step, Nick's alarm rose. His sons weren't in this house, but they had been. David's Dallas Cowboys hat that had been signed by the whole team was on the kitchen table. Their two school bags were slung over the arm of a kitchen chair.

And everywhere he looked, the sights made him recoil in horror. Shreds of duct tape that Hawkins must have used to bind his sons. A rope. Boarded windows. A broken lamp. Empty beer cans everywhere. And blood splattered on the front door. His stomach pitched.

"This is were he held them while he did no telling what to them." His voice broke with his resolve and he buried his head in his shaking hands. "Right here, not a good two hours from the house, and I couldn't find them."

Zach put a hand on his shoulder. "Haven't found them *yet*. We're not through, not by a long shot."

But Jake Hawkins or whoever had his twin sons had fled the area, not in the hunter's car but likely in some other vehicle he'd stolen. For some reason Nick couldn't fathom, the man must have given up on getting the ransom. If that were the case, there would be no reason for him to let the boys go free so that they could identify him.

He'd refused to think that the boys could be dead, but now the possibility hardened to cement in his gut. They might have found them in time if he'd let Zach call the shots from the beginning.

But he hadn't. He'd held out for the ransom attempt. He'd only wanted to protect them, but he might have destroyed them the same way he'd done his mother. He could have saved her if he hadn't waited until it was too late.

Becky was right to want the divorce. He didn't measure up. Cheering crowds, raving sports announcers and a huge bank account couldn't change that.

He walked over and picked up the cap David had been so proud of.

"Don't touch anything else," Zach said. "We need to preserve the evidence. There should be enough fingerprints in this room alone to put Jake Hawkins away."

"Then you're convinced Jake Hawkins is the kidnapper?"

"I'd stake my claim to my part of the ranch on it."

That was as sure as a man could get.

"He could be on his way to Mexico now," Nick conceded. But if he'd killed or even hurt David and Derrick, Nick would find him or spend the rest of his life trying.

"Let's get out of here, Zach. I need to give Becky the news."

*T*HE RAIN WAS FALLING *in sheets, and Becky's clothes were drenched, her skin numb from the wind and falling temperatures. "David! Derrick?"*

Why wouldn't they come? She'd been calling them for hours and, now she was lost in this pitch-dark forest. A low-hanging limb from a tree smacked her in the face when she tried to pass. Blood trickled down her cheek and across her lips. The metallic taste of it burned her tongue.

"David! Derrick? Answer me. I know you're out there."

A bird swooped down on her in the darkness, and its talons tangled in her hair. She fought it off, then tripped and fell on her face on the soggy ground.

A giant tarantula crawled across her hand. She screamed and knocked it away.

"Are you looking for us, Mom? We're right here."

She jumped to her feet and ran to them. When she reached them they were gone.

BECKY WOKE UP SHAKING. It took several seconds to realize that she was still in her car on the edge of the woods near Jake Hawkins's wrecked car. She rubbed her eyes and tried to clear the troubling remains of the nightmare from her mind.

She glanced at her watch. Eleven-fifty. She must have fallen asleep while waiting on the deputy who was supposed to drive her into Huntsville. The few minutes she was supposed to wait for a ride into Huntsville had lasted for two hours.

If anything, there were more cars here now than when she'd drifted off. But the action was no longer centered on Jake Hawkins's wrecked car. In fact, there was no one around it. The activity was in an area of bright lights shining through the trees off to her left.

She lowered her window. The rain had stopped. The wind had died down, as well. She opened the door, got out and started walking toward the lights and din of voices.

Someone grabbed her by the arm. She turned to find the young deputy she and Nick had talked to earlier.

"I'm sorry, Mrs. Ridgely, but you can't go back there. Crime scene. Secured area. You know how it is."

"Is there new evidence?"

"Yes, ma'am. One of the deputies had gone to take a—well, you know because there aren't any bathrooms around."

"I understand." She could use some decent facilities herself. "What did he find?"

"Two bodies."

"Two bodies." She swayed, and the ground started rising to meet her face.

The deputy steadied her. "It was those hunters that were missing. It was their bodies that were found. I'm sorry. I should have said that first. No excuse, but it's been a night."

She still wasn't sure she'd heard him right. "Did you say that someone killed Hermann Grazier?"

"Yes, ma'am. Killed him and his brother-in-law. Shot one of them in the back of the head, the other in the front. Real nasty."

"Jake Hawkins must have killed them."

"I'm not at liberty to divulge any information. If I did, it would just be supposition."

But who else would it be? Surely he hadn't killed

them for a phone. Only someone who'd gone totally mad would commit such an act.

The totally mad person who had her sons. The depths of her soul started to shake. She needed to get out of here.

"Would you tell Deputy Steve Jordon that I'm feeling much better now and that I'm going to drive myself back to Whistler's Inn in Huntsville? And if either my brother Deputy Zach Collingsworth or my husband Nick Ridgely shows up, you can give them that same information."

"I'll do it."

She'd call Nick when she got back to Huntsville, but not until then. He'd only insist she wait for him to drive her. She was fully capable of doing that herself now that she'd had some sleep and a new shock to steel her mind.

The deputy stayed at her side. "Do you know how to get back to the main road?"

"Probably not. Can you point me in the right direction?"

"Do you have a compass in your car?"

"There's one with the GPS system."

"Then keep turning to the west. I think it's about four turns before you reach Highway 190. That will take you right into Huntsville."

"Thanks." She hurried back to her car. Two people were dead. Nothing about this could be good. She turned the key in the ignition. "O, Holy Night" was playing on the radio. The clock said ten past midnight.

It was Christmas Eve.

THE FIRST THING Nick noticed when he and Zach returned to the spot where he'd left Becky was the action taking place in the nearby woods. The second was that Becky's car was missing. "I thought Steve Jordon was going to drive Becky back to the hotel in his squad car and leave her car for me."

"He was, but he may still be here. Judging from the lights and the crowd and that new strip of bright orange tape going up in the trees, I'd say they've uncovered some new evidence."

Which meant that Becky had probably given up on her ride and driven back alone. He pulled out his cell phone and was punching in her number when a young deputy stuck his head in the window Zach had just lowered.

"Mrs. Ridgely left about ten minutes ago, maybe less. She said to be sure and tell you that she got some sleep first and that she was wide awake. Said she was driving into Huntsville."

"Thanks," Nick said. "Did she seem all right?"

"Seemed as coherent as any of us, not that that's saying much."

Zach turned toward the site of the lights and action. "What's going on in the woods?"

"We found those two hunters who went missing— Hermann Grazier and Bruce Cotton. Well, to be more specific, we found their bodies."

They listened to the gory details. Zach interrupted with questions several times. Nick's mind had jumped ahead to terrifying conclusions. Number one was that Jake Hawkins was capable of murder.

"Never seen a man more eager to get back to prison." Zach stepped out of the car and tossed Nick his keys.

"Why don't you take my truck and go join Becky? I have a feeling she needs your company and that you need hers."

Nick nodded. "What about you? You need some sleep."

"I'll get some, but I want to take a look at exactly what they found. Steve or one of the other deputies will give me a lift into town when we're done. I'll get my keys from you over breakfast in the morning."

"That'll work."

Nick drove away from the scene, glad the rain was over, and thinking of his sons.

Memories of the night the boys were born sprang to life as if it had been yesterday. He'd been overcome with emotion the first time he'd held them in his arms— David in the right one, Derrick in the left.

He was certain his life had changed forever at that point. He was a father, a husband, a second-year player in the NFL. Finally he'd be able to bury the past and lose the insecurities and guilt that drove him.

He'd been wrong, of course. If anything the secret life of Nick Ridgely pushed him even harder to prove himself after he'd become a father.

Now he might lose his career and his marriage. And if that weren't terror enough, his sons were with a sociopath who'd already killed today. And that was the best scenario.

He beat a fist against the steering wheel as he pulled onto the rain-slick road. His day of reckoning had come.

HOURS OF POURING RAIN had left the old rock and dirt roadbed formidable and the shoulders a slimy sledge. Becky crept along, afraid to drive faster than a crawl.

She'd made one turn. Now her eyes were peeled for the next crossroad.

She hadn't realized earlier how narrow the roads were or how isolated they felt. Nick had been driving then, and she'd been consumed with the prospect of seeing Jake Hawkins's car and determining for certain if the shoes inside belonged to her sons. That seemed days ago.

So did Nick's shocking confession of a past she'd never even suspected. Even now, she struggled to fuse the Nick she knew with that frightened little boy who'd been forced to deal with issues far beyond his years.

The Nick she knew was driven, cocky, sexy. She'd fallen so hard for him when they met that she'd have married him that very night. Nick had been the sane one, insisting that they take it slow.

Not that they had in the lovemaking department. They'd been dynamite together—until football season started the following fall.

Even then he'd been driven to be the best player on the team. She'd accepted his ambition without question, considered it a good thing. She'd been far too in love with the star of the Longhorns to ever find fault with him.

But never once in all the years they'd been together had she seen the haunting pain in his eyes that had been there today when he'd told her about his mother's death. Had he hidden his vulnerability that well all those years or had she just been too blind to see what was in his soul?

She'd been quick to blame Nick for their lack of emotional attachment, but now it seemed that she'd been as guilty as he was of not seeing beyond the superficial. She'd never bothered to look beyond the facade of the man he appeared to be to see the person deep inside.

Now it all came down to the fact that neither of them had ever really known the other.

He wanted to change. Maybe she needed to do some soul searching and some changing, as well…when this was over. When their sons were safe.

Her car went into a skid as she rounded a sharp curve that sent her straining against her seat belt and the beams from her headlights jutting across a patch of dark woods. She tensed but managed to keep the vehicle from leaving the road.

Going even more slowly now, she caught a glimpse of movement on the edge of the illumination from her headlights. Her heart slammed against her chest as the earlier nightmare flashed across her consciousness.

She braked slowly and stared into the pitch blackness of the moonless night. She was overreacting. The movement had most likely been a deer or several of them. She'd hit a huge buck once driving back to the ranch after a function in Houston.

A heavy fog had drastically reduced visibility, and by the time she'd spotted the animal, it had been too late to stop. Just as she reached it, it had darted across the road. Her car had been totaled. Luckily she and her mother, who was dozing in the passenger seat, only suffered a few bruises.

Becky lowered the window. The night seemed eerily silent at first, and then she became aware of the cacophony of sounds made by the wind in the trees and myriad nocturnal creatures that flew through the branches and scurried through the grass.

Her finger was on the button to raise the window when she saw movement again. Not a deer but a person. She was almost sure of it—unless her mind was playing cruel tricks on her. After the past few days, that was entirely possible.

She got out of the car, rounded the back of it and stepped from the road into slush. "David! Derrick!"

The feeling of déjà vu was incredibly strong and frighteningly ghostly. It was the earlier nightmare all over again, only she was fully awake. She shivered as she took a few steps toward the thick growth of trees just feet from the road.

"David. Derrick. It's Mom."

A gust of wind slapped her in the face and jolted her from the harrowing state of hypnotic absurdity she'd fallen into. The constant stress was driving her over the edge. Her sons were with a kidnapper, not wandering the forest like spooked fawns.

She turned to walk back to the car, then stopped. Someone was here. She could hear whistling.

Chapter Fourteen

Footfalls sounded behind Becky. She spun around as a brawny arm locked her in a stranglehold.

"Jake Hawkins?"

"Yeah, but we're about to be real friendly, and my friends call me Bull."

Becky tried to break free of his hold, but a sharp prick at the base of her neck stopped her. He had a knife. One jerky move and her jugular would be sliced.

"Where are my sons?"

"Where I left them. Bleeding. Crying for their momma."

She fought the rush of panic and fury that shook her. She'd never hated another person, but she did now.

"Why? Why us? Why David and Derrick?" Her heart cried into her words. "We did everything just the way you said. We had the money. You didn't show up to get it."

"You called in the authorities."

"We didn't."

"Don't lie, you bitch. The cops swarmed my wrecked car like a hive of killer bees." He spit the words at her.

He knew. There was no use in lying. Less use to

fight as long as the knife was at her throat. "We only called them after you didn't show up as planned. We thought you no longer wanted the money."

"Like you'd know about wanting money. You living the friggin' dream life of a princess. Texas royalty. You like that, don't you? You always did."

"I don't know what you're talking about."

"High school, Becky. I'm talking Colts Run Cross High School. You parading around the football field in that cheerleading outfit that barely covered your behind. Wearing that stretchy top so that your young tits taunted every guy who passed."

"That was years ago, Jake. I wore the uniform they gave us. I didn't mean to taunt anyone. I barely knew you."

His grip tightened, and he lifted the arm under her chin, pulling her head back until she was looking up into his snarling face. "You didn't want to know me. You acted like I was dried-up paint on the wall until you started your nasty rumors. You liked thinking of me as a murderer, but you didn't know the half of it."

"That's not true. I never thought you killed your grandmother. I didn't." Not until now.

"The woman nagged me all the time. Told me I was as worthless as my tramp mother. Said I was a curse to her."

Becky fought to swallow against the pressure on her neck. "I'm sorry, Jake. I am. I didn't know."

"You didn't know. You didn't care. And now I don't care, either, not about you or your bratty kids. Not about Nick Ridgely, either."

Her face was so close to his that even in the dark she

could see the rage in his eyes. The same fury he must have felt when he'd pushed his grandmother down those stairs. When he'd pulled a pregnant woman from her car and stabbed her with a pocketknife. When he'd killed two men for no reason at all.

But she couldn't give up. They'd find her body, but would they ever find David and Derrick in time?

"Nick has the money, Jake. Let me call him, and he'll bring it to you," she pleaded. "All five million, in small bills, just like you said. You get the money, and you give us back our sons."

"Where's your phone?"

"In my handbag. I left it in the car. I'll get it and call him."

"Sure you would, right after you drove off and left me here."

"No. You can go to the car with me." Anything to give her a chance to get out of this alive.

"One call, Becky. One chance. If anything goes wrong, I'll kill you along with your sons and then wipe Nick Ridgely's face in your blood."

She would have gladly given him the money, only Nick didn't have it on him. It was back at Jack's Bluff. He'd be here in minutes if she called, but she had to keep him from walking into a trap.

"Nick will want to know where the boys are. He'll want to talk to them."

"Haggling won't work, Becky. You lost all the pawns in the game the second my knife touched your flesh."

Jake pulled her into the clearing and started to drag her toward her car. The lights from an approaching car stopped him. He yanked her back into the trees, the knife piercing her skin as he did. She felt only a quick sensation and then the hot, wet trickle of blood dripping from her neck.

A pickup truck pulled to a stop behind her car. The beams from its headlights sent a muted whisper of illumination through the trees. Jake's right hand stayed around her neck, but he pulled the knife away and exchanged it for a pistol.

"Make one sound and you're dead."

She had no doubt he meant the threat. But if she stayed silent and the driver of the truck walked toward them, he'd be the one who was dead, shot just as Hermann Grazier and Bruce Cotton had been.

A man stepped from the driver's side of the truck and walked to her car. Her heart jumped to her throat and sent agonizing stabs of dread through every fiber of her being.

The driver of the truck was Nick

NICK STARED into Becky's empty car. Her keys were in the ignition. Her purse was in the passenger seat. Her jacket had been slung to the backseat. He struggled for some positive spin to put on the situation, but there was none.

Trepidation gave way to full-scale alarm. He peered into the darkness on either side of the road and then went back to the truck for a flashlight. He shot the bright beam into the trees, searching for a sign of Becky, though he couldn't imagine any reason that she'd have ventured into the heavily forested area.

He fervently wished that he hadn't given the weapon back to Zach when they'd left the cabin where the kidnapper had been holed up with David and Derrick, but he'd had no idea that he'd need one tonight.

Muscles clenched and adrenaline pumping, he stepped off the road and toward the trees, shining the beam toward the ground to search for Becky's trail. He found it quickly, imprints of her boots carved into the muddy clay.

"Becky!"

No response. Yet he was sure she'd come this way. Or been lured this way. He called her name again, louder, panic adding a crusty crack to his voice.

Something rustled the grass to his left. He took off running toward the sound.

"Don't, Nick. It's Jake. He has a gun."

Too late. Nick saw Becky being thrown to the ground and Jake Hawkins's heavy foot stamp down on her stomach. The gun in his hand was pointed at her head.

"I want my five million, Nick Ridgely, and I want it now."

This was crazy. Becky surely hadn't come out here alone to meet the kidnapper. But she was here, a gun at her head. Nick had to think fast.

"The money's in my truck," he lied. "Let Becky go, and I'll get it for you."

"I don't like those rules. Let's try mine. You bring me the money, and I'll let your bitch live."

He obviously didn't want to risk coming out of the clearing for fear an armed deputy might come along as Nick had. That was Nick's only advantage.

"Drop the gun."

"You're not giving the orders."

"Then shoot me."

"Nick, don't." Becky was crying and straining against Jake's killer hold on her. "Just go."

"Drop the gun, Jake, or get the money yourself."

"Get the money or she dies."

"Where are my sons?"

"Dead."

Becky wailed as if her heart were spilling onto the ground.

A blinding fury roared through Nick's veins along with the sure realization that Jake had no intention of letting either of them walk away from this alive.

"Your sons didn't cooperate, so I killed them, the same way I'll kill Becky if I don't have that money in my hand in thirty seconds. One."

Nick's past flashed before his eyes in living color. The red blood as his mother had drooped against him. The plum-colored dress Becky had worn on their first date. The baby-blue blankets they'd wrapped David and Derrick in the night they were born.

"The money, Nick, or do I just pull this trigger now?"

So who would it be in tonight's game? Nick Ridgely who let everyone down? Or Nick Ridgely, star receiver for the Dallas Cowboys. Great hands. Lightning speed. Amazing timing.

Or Nick Ridgely, his own man?

Nick took one more step toward the car, then turned, diving into the air in that unexpected split second and coming down on top of Jake. His left hand cracked against Jake's right one, sending the pistol flying though the air.

Jake recovered quickly, planting a fist into Nick's injured neck at the top of his spine. Nick went down in excruciating pain, then stumbled back to his feet. He swung at Jake and missed as Jake hammered him with another right punch to the center of his back and a left jab to his collarbone.

He was hitting the right spots to make the most of Nick's injury. Delivering blow after blow. Nick stumbled away, trying to get his balance. He spotted Becky clawing in the pine straw for the gun. "Get out of here, Becky. Now!"

Jake was at him again, fists pounding into Nick's neck and spine as he jumped on his back and dug his knees into his side as if he were riding a wild bronco. The pain was so intense, Nick was afraid he'd pass out or that the doctor's fears would materialize and he'd fall into a paralyzed mass.

It would take that for him to give up and leave Becky with this madman. He fought back, finally slamming his backside into a tree with enough force to shake Jake loose and send him sprawling to the ground. Nick backed away to catch his breath and regroup. Jake came up with a knife, the blade extended. He swiped it across Nick's chest, drawing blood.

Becky was still on her hands and knees in the mud. "Take the car, Becky. Get out. Please get out of here."

Jake sliced into him again, this time across the right thigh. Nick grabbed a broken limb from the ground and poked it into Jake's face. Jake howled but never slowed down, coming at Nick and knocking him to the carpet of pine straw that was fast turning red with his blood.

He was losing feeling in his arms and legs. His vision was blurry. In spite of all Nick's vows, Jake Hawkins was going to win.

And then a blast of gunfire exploded, and Jake Hawkins finally quit coming at him.

"Nick. Nick."

"I'm sorry, Becky. I'm sorry I let you down."

"You didn't. Oh, Nick, say you're okay. Please tell me you can move."

His brain was too hazy to know for certain if he was alive or dead and dreaming. He rolled over and spit out a mouthful of blood and what felt like a dozen teeth.

"I thought he'd killed you, Nick. I was so afraid."

Slowly the scene came into view. Becky was crying and pushing Jake's body off him. He pulled her into his arms with the last of his energy and lay in the mud with her tears running down his chest.

"Are you all right?" she whispered between sobs.

He wasn't all right. He might never be all right again. Neither would Becky. He'd failed them, and their sons were dead.

"I'll call an ambulance," she said.

"I think it's too late for that. He looks dead."

"I meant for you."

"Not yet." He couldn't bear to have her leave his arms.

They lay in the dark holding on to each other, her sobs open and honest, his tears a burn of moisture seeping from his eyes.

He didn't know how much time had passed before the flashing blue lights from a squad car lit the area. The cops Jake had been trying so hard to avoid. He managed to stand and help Becky to her feet. There wasn't a part of him that didn't ache.

"Nick. Becky."

The deputy was no surprise. You could count on a Collingsworth. "Out here, Zach."

Zach strode to them. "What the devil happened here?"

"I saw someone in the trees," Becky said, her voice shaking and drenched in heartbreak. "I thought it might be David and Derrick, that they could have escaped from the kidnapper and were on the run. It was Jake."

"And then Nick came along and shot him," Zach said, jumping to the erroneous conclusion. He offered Nick a high five. "Good work, man. I didn't even know you were carrying a gun."

"I wasn't. It was his."

Zach knelt and felt for Jake's pulse, making sure he was really dead. "I guess the boys were wrong. They thought they'd taken his only pistol. He must have stolen one from Hermann Grazier."

Nick shook his head to clear it. "What are you talking about?"

"Why don't I let your sons tell you?" Zach whistled and motioned to the car. The door opened, and David and Derrick jumped out and started running to them.

"Becky wasn't that far off," Zach said. "The boys escaped and came walking out of the woods to where the cops were stringing yellow tape a couple of minutes after Nick drove off."

Becky didn't wait to hear the rest of her brother's explanation. She was already rushing toward David and Derrick. The three of them literally collided, tangling in a boisterous three-way hug before they pulled her down on top of them.

Nick couldn't move that quickly, but he did pretty well for a guy with a few new contusions to add to his medical report. He fell gingerly into the tangle of arms, legs and unadulterated joy.

THE HOMECOMING for David and Derrick was everything anyone could have expected and more. Every light in the big house was on, and every single member of the Collingsworth family had been waiting on the front porch when they arrived.

The only lull in the celebration had occurred in the short period of time it had taken for Becky, Nick, David and Derrick to shower off the mud.

Now David and Derrick were holding court in front of the fireplace, drinking hot chocolate, munching on cookies and fudge explaining for at least the tenth time how they'd lassoed the kidnapper and used his own duct tape stunt to render him helpless and at their mercy.

It was three in the morning, and no one seemed to realize that they should all be in bed.

Nick was the only quiet one, and Becky was certain he was paying the price for tangling with Jake Hawkins. He looked as if it hurt to move, but he never complained. It wasn't his style, and just maybe that wasn't so bad.

Becky slipped unnoticed from the family room and went back to the kitchen for a glass of water. Lenora was standing by the range, wiping tears from her eyes with a Santa Claus towel.

"So this is where you disappeared to," Becky said.

"I needed some alone time to count my blessings."

Becky put her arms around her mother, enfolding her in a hug. "You always believed they'd come home safely, didn't you? I tried, but I never seem to have your faith."

"I've had years to work on it. And I believe in miracles."

"After tonight, I think we all do. But I was afraid, so

very afraid. And not only for the boys. I think the divorce may be a mistake, Mom. I don't think all the problems with our marriage belong to Nick."

"Tell your husband that, Becky."

"Tell me what?"

Neither Becky nor Lenora had seen or heard Nick come into the kitchen. Now that they knew he was there, Lenora slipped from Becky's embrace and left them alone.

Nick frowned. "If this is bad news, I don't want to hear it tonight. Let me have Christmas first. Give me the holiday with you and the boys before I have to come back down to earth."

Her moment of truth. She took a deep breath. "I love you, Nick. I don't know if I ever realized how much until I thought Jake Hawkins was going to beat you into a pulverized, paralyzed mess. But I knew it then, and I know it now. I admit our marriage needs work, but…"

Nick crossed the room, slowly, the pain evident in his every step. "Oh, Becky. I love you so much. I'll do whatever it takes not to lose you. I'll give up football and move back here to the ranch. I'll talk every night about feelings until you are sick of hearing me. I'll attend every school function the boys ever have, even spelling bees. Just say what you need from me to make this work, and I'll give it my best shot."

"That's just it, Nick. I don't want you to give up football for me. I don't want you to give up anything. Our problems are not all your fault. They never were. Both of us have to work on being honest with each other about our feelings. You can't hide behind your past. I can't hide behind my stubbornness."

He cradled her face in his bruised hands. "Are you saying you'll give us a chance?"

"As many chances as we need. I don't want to face life without you. I want to raise our sons together, have grandchildren, grow old in each other's arms. I want to love you for the rest of my life. I just want the marriage to be all that it can be."

He pulled her into his arms and then winced in pain.

She pulled away. "I'm sorry. I guess this isn't the night for you to crawl back in my bed."

"Just try to keep me out. But promise not to move—or breathe heavy." He kissed her lightly on the lips, a sweet promise of all that would come in the lifetime ahead.

"Merry Christmas, Mrs. Ridgely."

"Merry Christmas, Nick."

She wouldn't have thought there was a chance of it a few hours earlier, but Nick had called it right. This really would be the merriest Christmas of their lives.

Epilogue

Three months later

"I've never seen you so excited or secretive, Nick. When are you going to tell me what is going on?"

"I've already told you. It's spring. We're going on a picnic on the beautiful Jack's Bluff Ranch."

"Yeah, Mom. It's a picnic. Don't you get it?"

Nick stopped the truck and opened his door so the boys and Blackie could pile out of the backseat of the double-cab Dodge.

"This is the new me," Nick said. "Can't get enough of family time."

"There's more going on here. I just haven't figured it out yet. You're smiling like you just won the Super Bowl."

"That's because I have the old Becky back." He slipped his arm along the back of the seat and tangled his fingers in one of her loose curls. "The Becky who makes love like a wild woman."

She punched him playfully. "It's just that you're so thrilled to be back in the saddle again."

"You got that right, lady. And such a nice saddle. You

can take a Collingsworth off the ranch, but you can't make her give up those wild bronc-riding ways in the bedroom."

"I'm just a rancher's daughter at heart."

"And don't I know it."

She had to admit she loved the weekends on the ranch, like this one. It was good for the boys, too. But she was happy in Dallas, as well. She thought she could probably be happy anywhere now that she and Nick were getting along so well—both emotionally and physically.

It was as if they'd found each other all over again. And best of all, the problems with his injury were practically behind him. He'd gone back to the doctor yesterday, and he expected the doctors to give him full clearance to start getting ready for the upcoming season any day.

Nick had parked at the spot where the creek that criss-crossed the ranch bubbled musically over a bed of angular rocks. They'd come here on his first visit to the ranch and made wild, passionate love on a blanket in the grass. He'd called it their special corner of the ranch ever since. She liked the fact that they'd come back here today.

"Can we go swimming?" Derrick called, already racing to the water.

Becky climbed out of the truck. "No. It's not summer yet. The water's too cold."

"Then can we wade?"

"Cold feet won't kill them," Nick said.

"Okay, wade, but take off your shoes and socks and watch out for snakes."

"Ah, the joys of ranch life." Nick walked to the front of the truck and leaned against the hood.

"It's not so bad," she said.

"Not bad at all. I was just teasing you."

She started to pull the picnic basket from the back of the truck.

"Let's wait for the food," Nick said. "I need to talk to you about something."

His voice had grown serious. She felt a sudden tightening in her chest. "This isn't about the doctor's report, is it? Did you hear something today?"

"Actually, I did."

He'd gotten bad news. That's why he was smiling— to hide his anxiety. She'd said she wanted him to share all his feelings with her, but she wasn't sure she was up to this.

Becky walked to the front of the car and snuggled next to him. He circled his arms around her.

Finally she got up the courage to ask the dreaded question. "Was the verdict bad?"

"Could be worse. I have some mild ligamentous injuries that are healing. Nothing to keep me from playing again, though I might be at slightly more risk of future injuries."

She breathed a sigh of relief, though the possibility of his having a serious injury never went down easily. "So you can still play?"

"I can." He kissed the back of her neck. "I've decided that I'm not."

She turned to face him, unsure she'd heard him right. "You can't give up football. You love it. It's your life."

"It *used* to be my life. Not that I'm knocking it. I've had a great career. Football was my salvation, but I don't need it anymore, not the way I did. I want to move on to new challenges and I'd like to do that here."

"In Colts Run Cross?" She was having difficulty buying this.

"Here. On Jack's Bluff Ranch. On this spot where we're standing. Our hideaway. Don't you think it's the perfect place to build our dream house?"

"I love it, but…I don't see you as a rancher, Nick."

"Whew. Now, that's a relief. I have no intention of being a rancher. I've talked to the school board. They need a head coach for the Colts Run Cross high school football team. I'd like to take that job. Football has given me a lot. It's time I gave something back."

He nudged her chin so that she was looking into his gorgeous brown eyes. "It's taken me a while to get here, but this is what I want. I was hoping it's what you want, too."

"Pinch me, Nick. I'm sure I'm dreaming."

"How about I just kiss you instead?"

His lips took hers hungrily, the passion as consuming as it had been when she'd first fallen in love with him.

"I love you, Nick Ridgely."

"That's good, Becky, because there is something else I need from you to make me totally happy."

"Name it, Coach."

"A daughter."

With pleasure.

"Or two."

She could handle that.

"And another son."

Now he was pushing his luck.

"Maybe even another set of twins."

She covered his mouth with her lips, cutting off his words before he'd talked her into a whole football team.

* * * * *

*Mills & Boon® Intrigue brings you
a sneak preview of...*

Delores Fossen's Security Blanket

*Quinn "Lucky" Bacelli thought saving Marin Sheppard
would be the end of their dalliance. But then she asked
him for protection from her domineering parents. And
to pretend to be the father of her infant son...*

Don't miss this thrilling first story in the new
TEXAS PATERNITY: BOOTS AND BOOTIES
*mini-series available next month from
Mills & Boon® Intrigue.*

Security Blanket
by
Delores Fossen

The man was watching her.

Marin Sheppard was sure of it.

He wasn't staring, exactly. In fact, he hadn't even looked at her, though he'd been seated directly across from her in the lounge car of the train for the past fifteen minutes. He seemed to focus his attention on the wintry Texas landscape that zipped past the window. But several times Marin had met his gaze in the reflection of the glass.

Yes, he was watching her.

That kicked up her heart rate a couple of notches. A too-familiar nauseating tightness started to knot Marin's stomach.

Was it starting all over again?

Was he watching her, hoping that she'd lead him to her brother, Dexter? Or was this yet another attempt by her parents to insinuate themselves into her life?

It'd been over eight months since the last time this happened. A former "business associate" of her brother who was riled that he'd paid for a "product" that Dexter hadn't delivered. The man had followed her around Fort Worth for days. He hadn't been subtle about it, either, and that had made him seem all the more menacing. And she hadn't given birth to Noah yet then.

The stakes were so much higher now.

Marin hugged her sleeping son closer to her chest. He smelled like baby shampoo and the rice cereal he'd had for lunch. She brushed a kiss on his forehead and rocked gently. Not so much for him—Noah was sound asleep and might stay that way for the remaining hour of the trip to San Antonio. No, the rocking, the kiss and the snug embrace were more for her benefit, to help steady her nerves.

And it worked.

"Cute kid," she heard someone say. The man across from her. Who else? There were no other travelers in this particular section of the lounge car.

Marin lifted her gaze. Met his again. But this time it wasn't through the buffer of the glass, and she clearly saw his eyes, a blend of silver and smoke, framed with indecently long, dark eyelashes.

She studied him a moment, trying to decide if she knew him. He was on the lanky side. Midnight-colored hair. High cheekbones. A classically chiseled male jaw.

The only thing that saved him from being a total pretty boy was the one-inch scar angled across his right eyebrow, thin but noticeable. Not a precise surgeon's cut, a jagged, angry mark left from an old injury. It conjured images of barroom brawls, tattooed bikers and bashed beer bottles. Not that Marin had firsthand knowledge of such things.

But she would bet that he did.

He wore jeans that fit as if they'd been tailor-made for him, a dark blue pullover shirt that hugged his chest and a black leather bomber jacket. And snakeskin boots—specifically diamondback rattlesnake. Pricey and conspicuous footwear.

No, she didn't know him. Marin was certain she would have remembered him—a realization that bothered her because he was hot, and she was sorry she'd noticed.

He tipped his head toward Noah. "I meant your baby," he clarified. "Cute kid."

"Thank you." She looked away from the man, hoping it was the end of their brief conversation.

It wasn't.

"He's what…seven, eight months old?"

"Eight," she provided.

"He reminds me a little of my nephew," the man continued. "It must be hard, traveling alone with a baby."

That brought Marin's attention racing across the car. What had provoked that remark? She searched his face and his eyes almost frantically, trying to figure out if it was some sort of veiled threat.

He held up his hands, and a nervous laugh sounded from deep within his chest. "Sorry. Didn't mean to alarm you. It's just I noticed you're wearing a medical alert bracelet."

Marin glanced down at her left wrist. The almond-shaped metal disc was peeking out from the cuff of her sleeve. With its classic caduceus symbol engraved in crimson, it was like his boots—impossible to miss.

"I'm epileptic," she said.

"Oh." Concern dripped from the word.

"Don't worry," she countered. "I keep my seizures under control with meds. I haven't had one in over five years."

She immediately wondered why in the name of heaven she'd volunteered that personal information. Her medical history wasn't any of his business; it was a sore spot she didn't want to discuss.

"Is your epilepsy the reason you took the train?" he asked. "I mean, instead of driving?"

Marin frowned at him. "I thought the train would make the trip easier for my son."

He nodded, apparently satisfied with her answer to his intrusive question. When his attention strayed back in the general direction of her bracelet, Marin followed his gaze. Down to her hand. All the way to her bare ring finger.

Even though her former fiancé, Randall Davidson, had asked her to marry him, he'd never given her an engagement ring. It'd been an empty, bare gesture. A thought that riled her even now. Randall's betrayal had cut her to the bone.

Shifting Noah into the crook of her arm, she reached down to collect her diaper bag. "I think I'll go for a little walk and stretch my legs."

And change seats, she silently added.

Judging from the passengers she'd seen get on and off, the train wasn't crowded, so moving into coach seating shouldn't be a problem. In fact, she should have done it sooner.

"I'm sorry," he said. "I made you uncomfortable with my questions."

His words stopped her because they were sincere. Or at least he sounded that way. Of course, she'd been wrong before. It would take another lifetime or two for her to trust her instincts.

And that was the reason she reached for the bag again.

"Stay, *please*," he insisted. "It'll be easier for me to move." He got up, headed for the exit and then stopped, turning back around to face her. "I was hitting on you."

Marin blinked. "You…what?"

"Hitting on you," he clarified.

Oh.

That took her a few moments to process.

"Really?" Marin asked, sounding far more surprised than she wanted.

He chuckled, something low, husky and male. Something that trickled through her like expensive warm whiskey. "Really." But then, the lightheartedness faded from his eyes, and his jaw muscles started to stir. "I shouldn't have done it. Sorry."

Again, he seemed sincere. So maybe he wasn't watching her after all. Well, not for surveillance any way. Maybe he was watching her because she was a woman. Odd, that she'd forgotten all about basic human attraction and lust.

"You don't have to leave," Marin let him know. Because she suddenly didn't know what to do with her fidgety hands, she ran her fingers through Noah's dark blond curls. "Besides, it won't be long before we're in San Antonio."

He nodded, and it had an air of thankfulness to it. "I'm Quinn Bacelli. Most people though just call me Lucky."

She almost gave him a fake name. Old habits. But it was the truth that came out of her mouth. "Marin Sheppard."

He smiled. It was no doubt a lethal weapon in his arsenal of ways to get women to fall at his feet. Or into his bed. It bothered Marin to realize that she wasn't immune to it.

Good grief. Hadn't her time with Randall taught her anything?

"Well, Marin Sheppard," he said, taking his seat again. "No more hitting on you. Promise."

Good. She mentally repeated that several times, and then wondered why she felt mildly disappointed.

Noah stirred, sucked at a nonexistent bottle and then gave a pouty whimper when he realized it wasn't there. His eyelids fluttered open, and he blinked, focused and looked up at Marin with accusing blue-green eyes that were identical to her own. He made another whimper, probably to let her know that he wasn't pleased about having his nap interrupted.

Her son shifted and wriggled until he was in a sitting position in her lap, and the new surroundings immediately caught his attention. What was left of his whimpering expression evaporated. He examined his puppy socks, the window, the floor, the ceiling and the ruby-red exit sign. Even her garnet heart necklace. Then, his attention landed on the man seated across from him.

Noah grinned at him.

The man grinned back. "Did you have a good nap, buddy?"

Noah babbled a cordial response, something the two males must have understood, because they shared another smile.

Marin looked at Quinn "Lucky" Bacelli. Then, at her son. Their smiles seemed to freeze in place.

There was no warning.

A deafening blast ripped through the car.

One moment Marin was sitting on the seat with her son cradled in her arms, and the next she was flying across the narrow space right at Lucky.

Everything moved fast. So fast. And yet it happened in slow motion, too. It seemed part of some nightmarish dream where everything was tearing apart at the seams.

Debris spewed through the air. The diaper bag, the magazine she'd been reading, the very walls themselves. All of it, along with Noah and her.

Something slammed into her back and the left side of her head. It knocked the breath from her. The pain was instant—searing—and it sliced right through her, blurring her vision.

She and Noah landed in Lucky's arms, propelled against him. But he softened the fall. He turned, immediately, pushing them down against the seat and crawling over them so he could shelter them with his body.

⊚™ INTRIGUE

Coming next month

2-IN-1 ANTHOLOGY

SECURITY BLANKET by Delores Fossen

Lucky thought saving Marin would be the end of their affair.
But when she asks him to pretend to be the father of her
infant son, it's an offer he can't refuse…

HIS 7-DAY FIANCÉE by Gail Barrett

When Amanda is held at gunpoint in his casino it's up to Luke
to protect her – by pretending to be her fiancé! Yet could their
fake engagement put them in danger too?

2-IN-1 ANTHOLOGY

THE BODYGUARD'S PROMISE by Carla Cassidy

Clay West isn't happy about his latest bodyguard assignment,
protecting a Hollywood child star from an unknown menace…
until he meets the tiny starlet's sexy mum!

THE MISSING MILLIONAIRE by Dani Sinclair

Harrison's shocked to discover beautiful Jamie's his new
bodyguard. And Jamie's ready to risk everything to
protect him – even losing her heart.

SINGLE TITLE

THE VAMPIRE'S QUEST by Vivi Anna
Nocturne™

Vampire Kellen has come to the city of Nouveau Monde
to save himself. But fiery Sophie is about to cause
him even more trouble!

On sale 18th December 2009

Available at WHSmith, Tesco, ASDA, Eason and all good bookshops.
For full Mills & Boon range including eBooks visit
www.millsandboon.co.uk

 **INTRIGUE**

Coming next month

2-IN-1 ANTHOLOGY

HIS BEST FRIEND'S BABY by Mallory Kane

When ex-air-force man Matt's dead best friend's tiny son goes missing he is determined to save the child. But he didn't expect his attraction to widow Aimee.

THE NIGHT SERPENT by Anna Leonard

Lily is an ordinary girl. Until she's caught up in a murder investigation led by Special Agent Jon Patrick and learns she is being stalked by the Night Serpent.

SINGLE TITLE

MATCHMAKING WITH A MISSION
by BJ Daniels

McKenna can't keep her mind off brooding bad boy Nate. He's come back to town to bury his past – but McKenna is determined to get him back at the ranch by her side.

SINGLE TITLE

CAVANAUGH HEAT
by Marie Ferrarella

It's been years since top cop Brian Cavanaugh has seen his former partner Lila, but he's surprised to discover their chemistry is as hot as ever!

On sale 1st January 2010

Available at WHSmith, Tesco, ASDA, Eason and all good bookshops. For full Mills & Boon range including eBooks visit
www.millsandboon.co.uk

2 FREE BOOKS
AND A SURPRISE GIFT

We would like to take this opportunity to thank you for reading this Mills & Boon® book by offering you the chance to take TWO more specially selected books from the Intrigue series absolutely FREE! We're also making this offer to introduce you to the benefits of the Mills & Boon® Book Club™—

- **FREE home delivery**
- **FREE gifts and competitions**
- **FREE monthly Newsletter**
- **Exclusive Mills & Boon Book Club offers**
- **Books available before they're in the shops**

Accepting these FREE books and gift places you under no obligation to buy, you may cancel at any time, even after receiving your free books. Simply complete your details below and return the entire page to the address below. You don't even need a stamp!

YES Please send me 2 free Intrigue books and a surprise gift. I understand that unless you hear from me, I will receive 5 superb new stories every month, including two 2-in-1 books priced at £4.99 each and a single book priced at £3.19, postage and packing free. I am under no obligation to purchase any books and may cancel my subscription at any time. The free books and gift will be mine to keep in any case.

Ms/Mrs/Miss/Mr _____ Initials _____

Surname _____

Address _____

_____

_____ Postcode _____

Send this whole page to: Mills & Boon Book Club, Free Book Offer, FREEPOST NAT 10298, Richmond, TW9 1BR.